ANYTHING FOR YOU

ANYTHING FOR YOU

EROTICA FOR KINKY COUPLES

EDITED BY
RACHEL KRAMER BUSSEL

CLEiS
PRESS

Published in the United States by Cleis Press, Inc., 221 River Street, 9th Floor, Hoboken, NJ 07030

Printed in the United States.
Cover design: Scott Idleman/Blink
Cover photograph: Luc Beziat/Getty Images
Text design: Frank Wiedemann

First Edition.
10 9 8 7 6 5 4 3 2 1

Trade paper ISBN: 978-1-57344-813-0

E-book ISBN: 978-1-57344-827-7

Contents

INTRODUCTION: AS KINKY AS THEY WANT TO BE

My wife is on her knees." That is how the first story in this book, "Like Riding a Bicycle," by Lisabet Sarai, starts off, and in some ways, it's why I don't think I even need to introduce these stories, although I am about to. What I like most about this book is that its authors, in each of these nineteen titillating stories, assume that the reader is already aware of the world of BDSM. That's not to say that if you're a curious newcomer to the world of bondage, discipline, sadism and masochism you shouldn't keep turning the pages, but just to point out that there is an ease with which these couples embrace their love of kink, in its varied forms, even when they are uneasy about the particular acts they are about to engage in. That push/pull, love/hate relationship with what turns us on is part of the beauty of BDSM and is a recurring theme here. In the course of these erotic vignettes, you will indeed learn about why, say, someone would want to be "forced" onto her knees, or bent over a bed or used as a plaything.

In these stories, you will find pain, and pleasure. You will find service and devotion. You will find Masters and Mistresses and curious onlookers—and so much more. You will find a dinner party where food is used for foreplay, and learn what CFNM stands for (hint: Clothed Female, Naked Male). But more than any particular scene or setup you'll read about—and they are quite dazzling in their ingenuity—what stays with me the most from these stories is the longevity of the couples, the way they can read each others' moans and sighs and screams so well, discerning a lover's desires based on years of practice.

One of my biggest pet peeves about BDSM erotica is when a story leaps too quickly into the "action" and doesn't give enough insight into who the characters are, what makes them tick, what makes them want to be bound, gagged, stripped naked, exposed, ordered around—or be the one doing those things. In every one of these imaginative, racy stories, you will find out why each part of the couple is there, what they get out of their relationship, what pushes their buttons, what animates their kink. You'll find anal penetration, asparagus sex, an interview with a Mistress and her most eager slave, role-playing, spanking, bondage, exhibitionism and much more. Fantasies are fulfilled, sometimes on command, sometimes in ways their creators never could have foreseen. Most of all, though, what comes through is the passion, caring, and commitment these couples have for one another, the love behind (and alongside) the lust, which is what enables them to do all the wild, wanton things they do.

In the closing story, "Everything She'd Always Wanted," by Ariel Graham, you will see the word *fear* over and over; the protagonist, Gwen, also experiences her share of panic. Her journey deep into the world of a Dominant/submissive relationship is captured in expert prose. Graham writes, "She'd adapted quickly, something in her recognizing what she'd been searching for." When I wrote earlier that there's a comfort with the topic of BDSM, what I meant is precisely what is shown so dramatically and beautifully in that story. What happens in it is Gwen's idea, as the title suggests, but she is still nervous, wary, uncertain if her biggest fantasy is actually one she is capable of going through with. It's this very fear that drives her, that arouses her, that pushes her to keep going. *The only thing you have to listen to is David*, Gwen thinks to herself at one point. She has to take a leap of faith to get from here to there, and when she does, a whole new sexual world opens up for her.

The same could be said of the other characters, men and women, tops and bottoms, you'll read about in these pages. In a sense they all have to take a leap of faith and trust their partners to guide them, whether it's Dan in D. L. King's "Big Night," who gets a very special fortieth birthday party, or the narrator of Sinclair Sexsmith's, "The Guest Star," who watches as her girlfriend takes a new lover, or Jack in "New Games on a Saturday Night" by Teresa Noelle Roberts, who is used to girls who know their way around the business end of a paddle, but has what he thinks he knows turned on its head by a novice, Serena. For him, "the turn-on wasn't so much giving the pain as being trusted to give just the right amount of pain."

I hope these stories will move you as deeply as they've moved me. They are rich, varied and incredibly naughty. Many of them have made me wish I could slip inside the body and mind of a given character and act out his or her devilishly dirty delights. All of them have shown me just how powerful a force kink can be, how it can bring couples closer together and show them the true depths of trust and desire they can plumb.

Rachel Kramer Bussel
New York City

LIKE RIDING A BICYCLE

Lisabet Sarai

To GCS, of course

My wife is on her knees.

I peer over the top of the Sunday *Times*, admiring the elegant curve of her spine and the fullness of her ass. Late afternoon sun strikes glints of gold from her tawny curls, which are swept into a haphazard tumble on top of her head, leaving her neck naked and vulnerable. She sits back on her heels. Her palms rest on her bare thighs as she scans the titles on the bottom shelf of the bookcase. It's been a warm day, the windows are open and she's wearing nothing but an Amnesty International T-shirt and gym shorts. Her ample tits sway visibly under the loose shirt. My cock twitches at the sight.

"Jon? Have you seen our copy of *The White Hotel*? I promised I'd lend it to Clara."

Her face is earnest, her eyes narrowed behind her glasses and her lips set in a determined line that accentuates the creases at their corners. I don't mind; I have my own wrinkles and furrows, more extensive than hers. I figure that they are marks of success. We've made it this far.

She thinks I'm reading, that I haven't heard her. With a petulant little sigh, she turns back to the neat ranks of hardcover volumes. Her back arches a bit, thrusting her breasts forward, and blood races into my cock. In seconds, I'm fully hard. But that's not all. Power rises, too, the old sense of supreme control, surprising and delighting me. I haven't felt this in a long time.

Setting the paper down, I flex my fingers. I'm still strong, or as strong as I need to be. In the end, it's not physical strength that's important.

My wife kneels by the bookcase, unaware that she has adopted the position I taught her, so many years ago. She has, perhaps, forgotten. I will make her remember.

"Mariah!" She starts at my voice—not at the volume but at the tone. Plus I have called her by her secret name. Our friends and family, her colleagues, know her as plain Mary. Only in the shadowed world of our fantasies does she become Mariah.

I watch the emotions play across her familiar features: confusion, disbelief, a hint of fear. "Jon?" she begins. "What...?"

"Silence, Mariah. Do not speak unless I ask you a direct question."

"But..." She's beginning to understand, but she's still fighting the notion. I can see her mentally reviewing all the tasks she has remaining on today's to-do list.

"Did I ask you a question?"

"No...Sir." In that fraction of a second delay between "No" and "Sir," my heart sinks. What am I doing? Those days are gone. Then the honorific rolls off her tongue and my spirit soars. She remembers. My cock throbs inside my jeans. Her muscles relax. She bows her head, letting go of her rebellion, and I think for a moment I'll shoot right then and there, like the horny grad student I was when we met.

"Get over here, girl." My fifty-three-year-old, full-professor wife seems to not find the epithet as ridiculous as it sounds to me. She crawls across the carpet, grasping my intent almost before I do. Her lovely fat ass (about which she constantly complains) is in the air. Her breasts swing beneath her. She makes her slow way to my feet, then rises to her knees once again.

Her cheeks are flushed. A barely perceptible sheen of sweat dampens her forehead. A lock of hair has worked itself loose to curl seductively under her pointed chin. Her hazel eyes meet mine for an instant. I can read her excitement and uncertainty. I nod and give in to the smile twitching at my lips. She exhales the breath she's been holding and lowers her gaze, awaiting my next command.

Power burns through me, raw and smooth as a swallow of fine scotch. What shall I require next? I want to see her naked; should I tear her clothes off, cut them away, or make her strip for me? And then what? Alternatives fill my imagination, a delirious whirl of possibilities. I didn't plan this. I have no script.

I try to focus, to slow my own breathing and quiet my racing heart. Outwardly calm, inwardly quivering with arousal, I rise from my chair. "Stand up, Mariah."

She hastens to obey, stepping her feet apart and clasping her hands at the small of her back. I doubt it's even conscious. It seems that she's quicker to reclaim the old knowledge than I am.

Towering over her, I remove her glasses and set them aside, out of harm's way. Then I pull her shirt over her head and toss it into a corner. Her opulent breasts sag a bit more than they used to, but the plump nipples are as juicy and brazen as ever. Who'd believe they'd nursed a child? I can't resist the urge to give them a vicious twist. Mariah gasps but otherwise remains silent.

"No bra, slut?" I tip her face up to mine, reveling in her embarrassment.

"No, Sir. You told me to always be ready for you." Indeed, I had given her those instructions, a thousand years ago, when we were first discovering each other.

"Quite so. And are you wearing panties?" Without waiting for a reply, I stretch the elastic and push the shorts down over her ample hips. The rich scent of her pussy wells up from between her parted thighs. I slide one finger into her slick folds and wriggle it deep into her body. She shudders with the pleasure of it. Her knees go slack as she struggles to open her thighs and give me better access.

I snatch my hand from her cunt and slap her left breast. "Slut! A couple of simple commands and you're soaked." I suck on my finger, savoring Mariah's salty ocean flavor. "What a kinky girl you are!" I want to sink down and bury my face in the damp thicket of her pubic hair, to eat her until she writhes and screams. Not yet, though. My Dom's sense of timing is coming back, and I know this is too soon.

Instead, I turn her around and land symmetrical slaps on each of her asscheeks. "Into the bedroom. Now!" She scampers away like a kid.

I take my time undressing. With my rigid cock pressed against the zipper, it's not easy getting my pants off. I swell even more when I imagine her, bare-assed and waiting for me to use her.

Naked and barefoot, I pad into my office and retrieve the key to the toy cabinet from the locked drawer in my desk. I feel wild, crazy with lust. Young, too. How long has it been? Ten years? More? We started to slack off when Anne was born. Outrageous demands. Little sleep. No privacy with the *au pair* always around. And we were so busy with our careers. I made vice president. Mary got tenure. We never stopped having sex, but kinky scenes required more energy than we seemed to be able to muster.

As Anne grew up, went to college and then on to grad school, the notion of playing our old power games felt more and more absurd. Somehow we forgot the magic of complementary fantasy that first brought us together.

But you never really forget. It's like riding a bicycle. Get back on and the rhythms return. Your legs pump, transmitting power to the wheels. You achieve the impossible, balancing on the edge, letting the wind rush by as you speed toward your destination.

I enter the bedroom as quietly as I can, curious about what I'll find. I didn't give Mariah any instructions. What will she decide to do? I find her on the bed, with her face to the mattress, knees pulled to her belly and ass in the air, presented to me. One of my favorite positions.

The sight fills me with evil glee, but I make her wait. I approach the trunk where we hide our implements of torture and delight, tossing aside the pillows that disguise it as a window seat. The lock is stiff but eventually gives way. The lid squeaks a bit as I raise it. A choked exclamation comes from the figure on the bed. "Be still, Mariah," I command, putting as much steel in my voice as I can.

Inside—oh, what bounty! The warm, complex smell of well-cured leather that rises from the interior has a Pavlovian effect on me. My cock surges and my balls tighten. I fight against the urge to let go, to let the excitement carry me away. I've got to hold on, for Mariah's sake as much as my own.

I trail my fingers over the cuffs, the clips, the chains and the neat coils of rope. Hoods, gags, dildos, paddles, crops and floggers fill the chest like long-buried treasure. What shall I choose to torment and please my sweet, submissive wife?

I glance back at the motionless figure on the bed. The rose-colored lips of her pussy peek out between her spread thighs. Even from here, I can see them glistening with her juices.

"Any requests, slut?" I ask, mischief welling up to replace sentiment.

"No, Sir. Whatever pleases you, Sir."

I'd love to suspend her. I glance up to the ceiling, verifying that the hook I installed two decades ago when we bought the house is still in place. But the spreader might put too much strain on her arthritic hip, and without it, she'd move around too much. I take out the violet wand, remembering the trails of sparks I used to coax from her moist skin, the way they lit the darkened bedroom as she jumped and writhed. Better, perhaps, to start with something more basic, to ease ourselves back into the game.

Finally, I select two pair of plush-lined leather cuffs, a black velvet blindfold, a purple butt plug that looks like some obscene eggplant, and my favorite whip—the signal whip with the braided green-and-black handle, genuine kangaroo hide, Mariah's gift on our tenth anniversary. I toss the mask, cuffs and plug onto the bed and sweep the whip through the air. It emits a whistle and a gratifying "crack" before it lands on the bed. Mariah tries unsuccessfully to stifle her moan.

"You just can't be silent, can you?" The harshness in my voice surprises me and elicits a whimper from my cringing wife. "Do I need to gag you?"

"No—no, Sir, please don't do that. I'll be quiet, I promise." In fact, gags are one of Mariah's limits. They terrify her, as does anything related to suffocation. Still, it makes an effective threat.

"Never mind. I'm going to make you scream." I'm brusque as I slip the blindfold over her tangled curls. I fasten a pair of cuffs around her ankles. "Hands down by your sides." When she obeys, I cuff her wrists and clip her corresponding hands and feet together. "Too tight?"

"No, it's fine, Sir."

I pinch her butt, leaving a pair of livid marks on her pale skin. "Fine? I think maybe you're enjoying this too much." I dabble my fingers in her soaked cunt. Her muscles clench around me. I smack her butt with my other hand and she actually giggles.

"Oh, you're in trouble now, missy," I tell her, trying hard not to laugh myself. She winces when she hears the drawer open and the burp of the lube spurting into my hand. "Yes, that's right. I'm going to skewer your ass with a plug the size of Texas and then I'm going to whip you till you bleed. You won't be able to sit down for a week."

I proceed to make good on the first part of my threat, slathering the bulging purple device with slippery gel. It's about two inches in diameter at its widest point. I know that Mariah can take more—I buggered her with a bedpost once—but that was a long time ago. I rub the tapered end back and forth across her anus, working to relax her muscles. Then I push and twist at the same time.

"Aye!" she screams, as the fat bulb breaches her sphincter and settles into her rectum. "Ow!"

I don't wait for her to get used to the sensation. Grabbing the single-tail whip, I swing it once or twice, trying to get used to the heft. All at once I'm consumed with doubt. What if I really hurt her? An incompetent whipping could do serious damage.

I slash the thong through the air once more and slam it down on the bed next to her bare feet. Her toes curl as the force is transmitted through the mattress. I'm not sure I can really control where the stroke lands. The whip whistles and cracks above her head—threatening but ultimately harmless.

The pause becomes uncomfortable. I've lost the rhythm of the scene.

"Sir?" Mariah sounds tentative, questing. "Is something wrong?"

Anger and disappointment rise together. "What? Why do you ask, girl?" I growl. Tears actually prick my eyes, me, the big bad Dom. I should have known you can't bring back the past. But it seemed, for a while, like it actually might be possible to recapture the magic. It felt so very right...

"Well, you said you were going to flog me, Sir." Mariah's alto voice is strong and confident. She's not afraid to tell me, in her sub code, what she wants. She, at least, has no doubts.

"Are you trying to tell me what to do?" I roar. "Are you topping from below?"

"Of course not, Sir. It's up to you. You should do whatever pleases you." She sighs. The plug in her ass twitches. "I'm yours, Sir—yours completely."

It's scene-speak, I know. Mariah would never talk like this in ordinary life. Still, it touches me, because I realize she means it. She trusts me, still, to do what's right for us, to take her where she needs to go.

I raise my arm, suddenly strong. The whip swishes through the air, snaps and makes a perfect landing on her right cheek. A bright red line stitches across her creamy flesh. My cock throbs in response to her pitiful wail. Taking a deep breath, I land a powerful stroke on her other globe and survey its reddening wake.

Mariah chokes back her cry of pain. "Are you all right, Mariah? Is it too much?"

"No, Sir," she whispers. "Not at all."

She wants this. She wants me to whip her, to push her to the limit and beyond. I bring the single-tail down hard on her quivering flesh. She moans and jerks in her bonds as I paint her ass with a brilliant lattice of scarlet stripes.

I slash at her with the whip, again and again, focused and untiring. I'm in control now. I can see exactly where each stroke will land. Every so often I snap the tip against the base of the plug, making it vibrate inside her. Mariah yells and thrashes about on the bed. I don't need to ask how she is. I can sense it. She's here with me, deep in the moment, giving her all.

My cock torments me, swollen and aching. All at once I just have to be inside her.

The whip clatters to the floor. I kneel behind her raised buttocks, grab her hips and ram my rigid dick into her cunt. She's hot as a furnace, wet as rain. She arches her back to give me better access. I can feel the bulk of the plug, narrowing her already tight channel. My fingernails dig into the scored flesh of her ass. I know the pain only amplifies her pleasure. Each thrust bangs against the base of the plug, forcing it deeper into her bowels.

Mariah loves it. I know she does. I remember the first time I took her in the ass, not long after we met—her ecstasy, my wonder that she could trust me so much, so soon. I contemplate wrenching out the plug and replacing it with my cock, but her pussy just feels too damn good. She might be a mother—almost a grandmother—but Mariah's still sleek and tight, muscular and eager, everything a man could desire.

I fuck her as hard as I can, as hard as she wants. She opens to me completely. I'm amazed and humbled by her submission— not at all like the stern Dom I'm supposed to be. I want to take her to her peak before I let go, but I can't keep control anymore. Jizz surges up my stalk and floods her pussy while a wave of pleasure sweeps me away.

I rock against her as the convulsions recede. She massages

my softening cock with her inner muscles, milking the last drops of come. She hasn't reached her own climax, I realize—then I understand. She won't come until I give her permission.

I reach between her sticky thighs, seeking out her clit. "Mariah, baby, you can come now."

I feel the trembling start, deep in her cunt, growing until her whole body shakes. "Oh..." she sighs. "Oh, Sir!" I hold her close, her raw, striped ass hot against my belly, as she writhes. As the tremors subside, I yank the plug from her butt and she comes again, this time louder and harder, dislodging my limp cock and spattering semen all over us both.

Later, as she lies cradled in my arms, I wonder: Was this just a fluke? A one-time adventure? Or are we really going to begin again, those dangerous, intoxicating games we used to play? I kiss her hair and savor the soft, warm flesh pressed against me. I'm so grateful. I'm not going to worry about the future.

"Jon," she says, circling my nipple with her fingertip and sending little sparks to my cock. "You know, there are lots of things we never got around to trying..."

And just like that, she has me spinning outrageous, lurid fantasies—like some teenager.

BORROWER BEWARE

Heidi Champa

I looked through every drawer, but they were nowhere to be found. I resorted to sorting through the piles on the floor and the hamper in search of my favorite stockings. It was too cold outside to go to work with bare legs, and my last two pair of awful backup panty hose had runs in them. I needed my stockings, my perfect-fitting, black retro stockings with the seams, but they were gone. I had a sneaking suspicion about who'd taken them, but she was already long gone, too. I pulled a threadbare pair of leggings out of the pile on the floor and pulled them up my goose-bumped legs. They didn't look quite right, but there was no time to worry about that. If I didn't leave soon, I would be late. I vowed to confront Nikki, just as soon as she got home from work. It took all my strength not to call her immediately, but I knew this conversation was best done in person.

Not only did she saunter in almost an hour late, Nikki was wearing my stockings, proudly. They looked fantastic on her, especially when complemented by the just-an-inch-too-short

black skirt I'd bought her a few weeks back. I hated to admit
it, but she almost looked better in my stockings than I did. Her
young, pert legs begged to be covered with silk, and she acted
like she knew it all too well. I watched her as she hung up her
coat, wondering if the stockings were attached to my favorite
garter belt. She put her keys in the bowl by the door and finally
turned to face me. She smiled and looked so innocent, despite
the evidence being in full view. I returned her grin, not wanting
to pounce just yet. I wanted to bide my time, just a bit. Lay my
trap and let her fall right into it.

"Hey, baby, how's my pretty lady today? Did you miss me?"

"Fine, Nikki. How was your day?"

She sighed and sat on my lap, squashing me back into the
lounge chair I was sitting in. Planting soft kisses along my cheek,
she reached my lips and went to town, moving her sweet tongue
gently around mine until she was satisfied and pulled back. She
looked so sweet and innocent, but I knew better. Behind those
eyes was a ton of mischief, and that was one of the things I
loved most about her. Her stocking-covered legs rubbed against
me, the silky fabric caressing my now-bare legs. Damn, they felt
good. I couldn't resist running a finger along the seam, stopping
just above the hem of her skirt. My finger traced along a flaw
in the stocking, a small but distinct ladder that was starting to
grow. Nikki cooed, nuzzling my ear while I teased her, unaware
of my discovery. I decided it was time to go in for the kill.

"Those are really, really nice stockings. Where did you get
them?"

She froze, only for a moment, knowing she was caught.
Despite her best efforts to hide it, Nikki knew she had been
found out. She wasn't one to give up easily, but then again,
neither was I. I could tell she was going to lie before she opened
her mouth. Her face changed, her eyes averting from mine, just

like they always did before she told a big fib.

"Oh, I don't know. I think I bought them a while ago. They reminded me of yours, so I thought I'd get them. Do you like them?"

I laughed, moving my hand up to her neck, running my fingers through her hair. She relaxed back into my grasp, just in time for me to give her brown tresses a good yank. The yelp from her mouth sounded so cute, I gave her hair another pull, just for fun.

"Don't lie to me, Nikki. You are so lousy at it. Those are my stockings. I tried to find them this morning, but I couldn't. You know very well I told you not to borrow those stockings."

I let go of my grip on her hair so she could look at me. Her eyes were full of remorse and she tried to sound contrite as she apologized.

"I'm sorry, baby. I know you told me not to, but they're so pretty. I didn't think you would mind if I wore them just this once. Don't you like the way they look on me?"

She pressed a hand in between my legs and applied pressure to my clit. I let her do it for a few seconds, before pulling her hand away. I wasn't going to let her talk her way out of her punishment. It was the only way she would learn.

"They do look good on you, but that isn't the point. I needed them this morning and they weren't here. And now you've ruined them, haven't you?"

I turned her attention to the small defect in the back of the stocking near the lace cuff and her eyes widened in horror. I could tell she was waiting for me to yell at her, but instead I ran a finger along her cheek, still biding my time.

"So what are we going to do about this little problem, Nikki? I think it's time I taught you a lesson. What do you think?"

She swallowed hard before responding with a timid nod of

her head. Pulling her off my lap, I led her by the hand to the bedroom, her sweaty palm telling me she was just a bit scared. I started stripping her of her clothes, leaving the stockings and that perfect garter belt behind. The cool air in the house made her nipples peak, and when I moved my fingers over them, they tightened up even more.

"So, are you ready to take your punishment, Nikki?"

"Yes. I'm so sorry, baby. Please forgive me."

I smirked at her hollow apology, knowing that the real one wouldn't come until later. I turned her away from me and she bent over the bed without any prompting. On the surface, Nikki seemed well trained, but she was always pushing me. I knew she did it because she liked her punishments a little too much. That made two of us. Her ass looked so tantalizing up in the air like that. The thong she was wearing nestled enticingly between her delicious asscheeks. The two globes of creamy white flesh called out to me, and I had to answer. My hand hit her ass, and she gasped at the pain. Her forehead rested on our rumpled sheets as I peppered her with more and more swats, going back and forth between each cheek. Her moans started to sound more like cries, so I stopped, admiring my work.

The flush of her skin was nearly glowing, the red hue radiating heat when I touched it. I ran my fingers down her crack to her pussy, which was now soaking wet. I flicked each garter clip open, releasing the stockings from their confinement. I slid off her sodden thong and removed the garter belt from her waist. That just left my stockings, clinging beautifully to her thighs. I took my time sliding each one down and removing it from her long, gorgeous leg. It seemed only fitting to give my favorite stockings a proper sendoff, and I had a brilliant idea to put them to good use.

"Lie down on the bed, Nikki."

She obeyed me quickly, stretching herself out on the bed like a good little girl. Kneeling next to her, I took one skinny wrist at a time and tied it to the bed frame using the black-seamed silk as her bond. I tied her up extra tight, just to prove a point.

"Now keep those legs open nice and wide, Nikki."

"Okay, baby. I will."

My hands traced up her thighs with my fingertips, in no hurry to give my attention to her weeping slit. Starting at her knee, my tongue meandered up toward her pussy. Nikki tried to push her hips forward toward my mouth, but I continued on, licking down her other leg. She was already grumbling, despite my warnings for her to be good. I smiled, amusing myself with her torture. My fingers found her pussy lips, puffy and wet from arousal. That made her speak, even though she knew she wasn't supposed to.

"Baby, please. I need you."

I pressed my thumb to her clit while sliding my finger inside her and then pulling all the way back out. I licked my finger clean, just as she pulled her head up to look at me. A tiny gasp escaped her lips as she watched me. She looked sexier than any woman I had ever seen, her eyes pleading with me to give her what she needed. My moist finger slid back inside her, enjoying the tight, wet pull of her pussy. While I thrust slowly, I teased the tip of her clit with the pad of my thumb, applying just the right amount of pressure. Over and over, I plunged my finger inside her, taking my sweet time. She was practically whimpering for me to speed up, but I kept things at my pace.

"Do you want me to lick that sweet pussy? Is that what all the fuss is about up there?"

I knew she wanted me to, but I wasn't about to give in that easily. I wondered if she could manage to say the words out loud, but when she looked down at me, she seemed to know I wouldn't continue without them.

"Yes. Please, baby. Lick my pussy. Stop teasing me. I'm so

sorry. I won't wear your stockings ever again, I promise. Please, baby, please."

I smiled up at her as I thrust two fingers into her cunt. Finally, after several more agonizingly slow strokes, I ran the tip of my tongue over her, her clit throbbing at the contact. I closed my lips over the tender flesh, tugging her clit to rapt attention. She always tasted so good, and I couldn't help but moan as her essence hit my tongue. Sucking her hard nub into my mouth, I flicked it with my tongue, her hips thrusting up each time I made contact. I pulled back, looking up at my beautiful girl as I slowed my fingers down to a veritable crawl. Her eyes were closed tight, but once she realized I was staring, she looked down at me. I held her gaze as I laid a few small licks on her clit, not giving her too much, just enough to inch her ever closer to the edge. It was supposed to be punishment, after all.

I pulled my fingers from her cunt and reached them up to her pouty mouth. Rubbing the moisture onto her lips, I let her lick around each digit before plunging them into her mouth. Again, she closed her eyes as she licked my fingers clean, savoring her own flavor as she went. When I was satisfied, I removed my fingers and trailed them down her body, leaving behind a moist trail on my way back to her pussy.

"How you doing, Nikki?"

"Baby, I'm sorry I was so bad. I need to come. Don't make me wait anymore."

"Aww, someone is impatient. Maybe I should take pity on you."

"Please."

She begged so sweetly; I knew I couldn't make her suffer too much more. My fingers moved back inside her, the sounds of her sexy moans filling the quiet of the bedroom. I heard her pulling on her restraints as I put my tongue back to her hard clit and went to town, my poor stockings getting a workout from her once again. I held her unruly hips still, trying to regain control. I moved slow, then fast, my fingers and tongue furious one minute and plodding the next. Two fingers became three, four, stretching her open farther than she had been in months. I couldn't stop myself from moaning into her cunt, my own pussy becoming wet and needy. I resisted the urge to finger my cunt, having better plans for myself than that.

I could tell her orgasm was building inside her, but I backed off, leaving her restless and edgy for a few minutes longer. My fingers were out of her body, and I just stared at her, waiting for her to meet my eyes. As soon as she looked at me, I was back inside her, making a scream fly out of her mouth. I attacked her with my tongue, rubbing over her clit so fast she could no longer keep still. The heat, the explosion of her pleasure crashed so quickly, Nikki bucked off the bed, her hips moving violently. But I was relentless and kept up with her, and kept her coming for as long as I could. I didn't think she was ever going to stop, and honestly, I didn't want her to. As far as I was concerned, Nikki could keep going all night.

Finally, she lay spent, her arms hanging loosely in their captivity. I moved up her body, my knees on either side of her stomach. I moved to untie her, but stopped.

"Baby, please untie me. Haven't I been good?"

I moved my cunt close to her face, pausing a few inches from her pouting mouth. She tried to hide her smile, but couldn't.

"You've been pretty good, Nikki. But I think you still owe me, don't you?"

"Yes, baby. I do."

"Tomorrow, Nikki, we'll see about getting me some new stockings. And if you use that tongue right, I may buy you a pair of your own."

ANYTHING SHE WANTED

Neil Gavriel

It wasn't the first time she'd put her fingers in my ass.

A week ago, I'd have said that Samantha and I were mismatched, a bad fit, but then she put her fingers in my ass and I'd *very* quickly reevaluated.

We'd met at a mutual friend's costume party a few months back. She was the devastatingly beautiful blue-eyed wood nymph with leaves woven into her long brown hair and a cosmopolitan always in hand. I was the superhero who couldn't help but notice the way her too-short green silk dress clung to her slender body—accentuating an ass that was almost too perfect to be real—and who desperately wished he really did have X-ray vision (if only just for the night). Once I got a good look at those long, lean legs poured into shiny brown tights, my serious nylon fetish kicked in and I finally mustered the courage to speak to the dryad of my dreams.

Samantha and I talked for hours that night while the room faded into a dull hum around us. Despite the obvious mutual attraction and a shared love for great food, strong drinks and old movies, I figured we didn't stand a chance. Samantha was polyamorous and bisexual (and currently in a relationship— albeit a long-distance one—with a woman), while I'd pretty much been the poster boy for serial monogamy. One alcohol- lubricated night a month later I told her just what she did to me, but that me being monogamy boy meant it was a no-go. So, of course, a week after that we ended up making out in my kitchen at my twenty-seventh birthday party while giggling friends quietly excused themselves from the room; she'd batted those big blue eyes just a little too fetchingly when she'd asked for another cosmo, and I'd just had to pull her into my arms and kiss her. I didn't think we'd last, but I'd had to taste her lips, had to feel her body against mine.

And then, a week ago, Samantha put her fingers in my ass.

She'd made the happy discovery as she was expertly sucking my cock and her questing fingers brushed against my asshole. I parted my legs slightly, and she read the invitation. She slicked her fingers with lube from the bottle she kept in her dresser drawer, while I shivered in anticipation. She slid one finger inside, then another, and my groans of pleasure gave away my secret, that I'd been waiting for her to discover just how much I'd wanted those fingers in my ass.

Seconds later and I was trapped in that euphoric place, where I desperately wanted to come but just as desperately didn't want it to ever end. Her mouth on my cock was wet, slippery, insis- tent heaven; her fingers unstoppable; and I could only hold off my orgasm for so long. "I want you to explode in my mouth," she'd said, and so I did, my body convulsing, knuckles white as I clutched at the sheets of her queen-sized bed and took a deity's name in vain.

It shouldn't have surprised me, what she did, as our sex

life was never what you would call conventional. She discovered early on that I could talk dirty and, as she put it, "If you can talk, we can play." So our nights were spent with me weaving words of delicious and exacting filth in her ears while she would masturbate with her Hitachi Magic Wand. We'd lie side by side in bed, my left hand gripping her left wrist tightly, holding it above her head; her right hand nestling the head of the Wand above her clit while I traced patterns on the amazingly soft skin of her breasts and belly and stroked her ever-so-stiff nipples.

We'd play out the scenario that she found hottest, that I was forcing her to masturbate for me. She would ask why I wanted to see her do it, in increasingly desperate tones as her orgasm neared. I braided endearments with smut, telling her how beautiful she was, but then commenting on how slick her slutty little pussy seemed to have gotten, followed by saying how much I loved to watch her breasts as she arched her back in ecstasy. I would tell her how impossibly hard she'd made me, how much I wanted to lick the fine sheen of sweat off of her belly, and that if she didn't stop rubbing herself like a depraved whore I'd have no choice but to come all over her tits, massaging my semen into her skin and scooping it into her come-thirsty mouth. All of that was just buildup, though, really.

"Why?" she would plead, until finally I would stop teasing her and tell her what she really wanted to hear. "Because you don't have a choice," I would say, gripping her wrist harder to emphasize the point. "Because I won't fucking let you up until you come for me." She would come then, her body a live wire as she shook uncontrollably with pleasure.

After a moment to catch her breath, she would either take me into her mouth or unroll a condom onto my cock and guide me inside her and on top of her, telling me I could come as quickly as I wanted to while she pinched my nipples to bring it about just that much quicker.

Monogamous, polyamorous; whatever we were, Samantha and I had proven especially adept at finding those hidden fantasies that you hope a lover will stumble upon and offer as her own idea. I'd found hers when I'd whispered my first profane endearments, and she'd found mine when she'd slid those slippery fingers deep into my asshole last week.

It wasn't just the physical sensation of having her fingers inside me, which was, of course, hugely pleasurable; it was the frame of mind it put me in. Those magic digits flipped some switch, and I suddenly didn't have to be in control. I was calm, compliant and infinitely pliable. I wanted to do any and every thing she asked and was desperate for her to ask me to do something—the "naughtier" the better. In my head (because I was still too afraid to say the tacky un-PC words out loud when it came to my own pleasure) I would scream out, *Make me your little bitch! Call me your whore, anything! Just don't ever stop this.*

Tonight, with her mouth loving my cock and those fingers inside me once more, that voice in my head was loud enough that I almost didn't hear what she said.

"Have you ever had a girl use a strap-on on you?" she asked.

My heart raced and I tried to not sound too needy, too desperate. "No, have you got one?"

"Yes."

I didn't need to tell her that I wanted her to use it on me; she was pumping my cock in her hand and it was so hard she could have used it to cut diamonds.

"I think you'll need to be on your hands and knees for this," she said, getting up to fetch it from the same drawer that held the lube. She quickly stepped into a harness with the efficiency of someone who'd worn one many times before. I wondered how many women she'd used it on. I wondered if I was the first man. Her back was turned to me as she quickly buckled the straps.

"Close your eyes," she said, and I obeyed. I heard her soft footsteps and then felt her hand in my hair, ruffling it before she grabbed an insistent handful.

"I need you to suck on this now. Will you suck on this for me?"

"Yes, Mistress," I said. She hadn't asked me to call her that ever, but I heard her sharp intake of breath as I said the word and knew I'd stepped up appropriately to the game she was offering. I'd wanted to call her that since she'd first violated my backside, but was afraid. Now I knew I didn't need to be, that everything was okay, nothing forbidden.

"Ask for it," she said.

"Please, Mistress, may I suck on your..." I hesitated.

"Cock," she said, simply. No equivocating with that word, no softening by suggesting *dildo* or *phallus*. She meant business.

"Please, Mistress, may I suck on your cock?" I said quietly.

"Oh, yes, you may. Open your eyes now."

I'd expected something silver, or purple—feminine in some way—but it was realistic as all hell, veined and pink and replete with lovingly rendered rubber testicles.

I looked up at her for guidance, or permission not to do it, or something to save me from myself, and she gave me a little smile and a wink, and then she fed the cock to me, sliding it in between lips that had lost the power to resist about ten minutes back.

I raised my hand to grab the cock, to control its invasion of my mouth, but she slapped my face lightly. "No, no. Only your mouth."

The last few weeks had been a master class in oral sex (at least receiving it). Samantha found vaginal intercourse a little painful unless extremely turned on (my dirty mouth being key to helping out there), so she'd vowed long ago that she was going to give blow jobs like she'd invented them. She'd made good on that vow (and how!) and even the simple act of innocently pulling that long brown hair into a ponytail (something she ritualistically did before that first lick or stroke) was enough to get me instantly hard (embarrassingly so that time we'd been at the outdoor market and she'd just wanted to get her hair out of her face).

It was a lot to live up to, but I gave it my best effort, incorporating all of her/my favorite techniques. I pulled back to lick and nibble at the underside before engulfing the head in my mouth again and she smiled the smile of a teacher to a prize pupil. She cooed encouragements at me while she held my hair in her fists, telling me to relax my throat so she could fuck my face harder. "Deeper. Hold it there. Christ, your mouth has needed my cock in it," she said, gagging me just a little as she took my face for her pleasure, each thrust increasing the dildo base's contact with her clit. She let go and let me suck at my own pace while she languidly raised her hands to her breasts and lightly brushed her open palms over her hardened nipples, licking each palm in turn before rubbing the wetness on her sensitive nubs. I took it as high praise when she finally moaned softly and said, "You're such a fucking good cocksucker, baby."

I glowed with pride and redoubled my efforts, happy that I was getting the hang of the relaxed throat thing and she was penetrating my mouth deeper. She stopped after a time, saying, "I know you'd like to suck my cock all day long, but I have other plans for this." She pulled her cock from my pursed lips with a small pop and unrolled a condom on it and started lubing it with the little bottle from her dresser.

It's one thing to fantasize about it, to dream of what your

girlfriend would do with your ass if she could only read your dirty mind, but it's another when you're faced with seven inches of pink reality strapped to her pelvis. She noticed my eyes growing bigger and put a hand on my cheek to calm me.

"You're going to love this, I know it," she said.

"It'll change everything."

"Well, maybe I should stop, then," she said, calling my bluff.

I spluttered for a moment, and she laughed a rich, silvery laugh.

"Turn around now, I think I need you to be my little bitch," she teased.

I couldn't make eye contact with her anymore and my cheeks burned with shame, but I was painfully hard. I turned around, still on all fours, and faced the sea of pillows at the head of her bed. I reached out to grab one, and she spanked my ass, hard.

"I think we've already determined that I'm calling the shots here. I'll decide if your comfort is of any concern to me or not."

"Yes, Mistress," I said, still feeling that little thrill whenever I said it.

"Ass up, head down."

I did my best, raising my ass high and stretching my arms out in front of me while lowering my head to the bed, as if in supplication to some wonderful, kinky god. Something clicked for me at this point, as I felt her fingers lubing my asshole anew. I was exposed to her—body and soul—and she loved it. She was in control of me and I trusted her implicitly. I lowered my head farther, as if the bed were a pool of her desires and I could subsume myself completely to them by burying myself in the cool sheets.

She pushed the head of her cock into me just a little bit, but stopped when I whimpered.

"Do you need me to go slower, slave?" she said.

A shiver ran down my spine as she said that word; it was a potent almost-cliché that carried just the perfect resonance for me. "No, Ma'am, it's just...intense." I remembered the first time a girl had sucked me off, how I'd lost all sensation in my extremities as my world had narrowed down to her mouth and my cock. I looked back at Samantha, not wanting to get lost like that right now. Her eyes were suddenly hard, almost cruel, as she slid deeper inside me.

I couldn't help myself and cried out, "Oh, god."

She was slow but insistent, pushing her cock inside me. I felt impossibly full and there was still more to go. Finally, I felt the straps of the harness against my asscheeks and the rubber testicles of the dildo. I heard a click and then felt the dildo vibrate gently inside me, which caused me to groan.

"Do you like this, little bitch?" she asked.

"Yes. Fuck. I feel impaled."

"Do you want me to fuck you with this dick in your ass?" She moved in and out of me with the tiniest of movements, but it rippled through me like a series of waves from a skipped stone.

"Yes, please." I said.

"Please, what?" she said.

"Please fuck your little bitch with your dick," I begged.

And she did just that, slowly at first, very slowly, stretching me more, each vein and bump on the rubber dick in my ass causing little whorls of pleasure. She sped up when she sensed I was ready for it, reading my body language with amazing skill. We soon became a well-oiled carnal machine, groaning with each delirious stroke.

I looked back over my shoulder, wanting to see the face of the woman I loved as she buggered the hell out of me. She was massaging her breasts, rolling her hard nipples between her fingers with eyes closed and lips parted. I perched up on my hands to get a better look at her and snapped her momentarily out of the spell. "This isn't for you," she said, and leaned forward and roughly pushed my cheek until I was facing forward again. The image was burned into my brain forever, but she knew it was torture that I couldn't watch her this time. All the while, she slowly and relentlessly slid in and out of me, fucking me with her cock.

Eventually, after a time that seemed both forever and all too short, she fell onto me, biting my neck and back. I could feel her hard nipples on my back, our sweat mingling, and the sensation was almost enough to push me over the edge.

"I'm going to come now. You need to fucking come for me, slave." She reached down to stroke me, and, as the telltale signs shook her body, gripped my cock hard and pumped it. I came with her, as hard as I'd ever come before, screaming out that I loved her as I did.

We collapsed onto the bed, and she whispered in my ear that she loved me, too. After a few moments, I pulled myself off of her cock and lay on my back, holding her in my arms. We didn't talk just then; we knew we'd taken some big steps and needed time to process them. We kissed for a while and her hand trailed down to play with my spent but happy cock.

"That," she said, "was fun. I didn't think I'd get off on it so much, but I liked you helpless and supplicating before me. You'd do anything I wanted, wouldn't you?"

"Absolutely anything, Mistress," I said, smiling, but meaning it. It struck me then that what she'd just said wasn't a question. She'd really always been in control of everything. When I was holding her down and talking dirty to her, it was what she wanted. When she fucked me with her fingers and told me to come, it was at her bidding. When she made me beg for her cock in my ass, it got her off. I realized I was pretty happy with that and didn't want it any other way. "Anything at all."

"I think I might have to invite a friend over next time we do this," she said, and I could hear a little giggle in her voice.

"Oh, really?" I said, still smiling. In my head, I saw Samantha and another woman, forcing me to service them with my tongue, taking turns fucking my ass with strap-ons. I imagined myself kneeling at their feet while they completely ignored me, a happy voyeur to two women pleasuring each other with lips and fingers and toys from Samantha's dresser drawer. I wondered if it would be her friend Jennifer, the redhead with the creamy white skin, or maybe Samantha's girlfriend Trina. I pictured Trina flying back from London, discovering me trussed up at Samantha's feet on their apartment floor, an abject plaything offered as a welcome home gift.

"Yes, I think I'd really like to see you suck his cock," she said.

I could claim (truthfully) that I was straight. I could claim (also truthfully) that I'd never fooled around with a guy before. But her hand was on my cock, and she felt it stiffen at her words, and I couldn't claim that I didn't want to be at her feet doing just what she described. How could I resist? She already knew my secret by then. She knew that I would do anything she wanted.

TAILS

Deborah Castellano

We had just finished eating a romantic dinner in and he was doing the dishes while I packed up what remained from our strip steak dinner. I had just finished up the last of my glass of merlot and was contemplating whether or not to start on the amaretto ice-cream balls we had made earlier when I got a better idea.

"Heads or tails?" I asked. He grinned at me.

"Heads," he said.

I flipped the coin. "Tails," I said, smirking at him. "Your tail!" I swatted his ass.

He sighed theatrically as he put the last dish in the dishwasher. "The things I do for you, Daddy."

I could already feel myself getting wet just from him saying the magic word. *Daddy.* Grabbing his hand, I pulled him to the bedroom. Strolling over to our bed, I reached under it to pull out the black satin sheet we always used for our more serious play. I spread it out over our bed while he shut off the bedroom light, then he lit the Midsummer's Night candles that I couldn't ever get enough of. When I turned around, he had already wiggled out of all of his clothes.

"Naked already?" I asked with amusement. "Such a little slut." He preened and pranced over to the bed like a high-stepping pony to slide my soft gray yoga pants off of me and then took down my hot-pink panties that framed my ass so perfectly. Raising my arms, I allowed him to peel me out of my pale pink camisole top and matching push-up bra. He sat at the foot of the bed while I nestled into the mountain of throw pillows I'd insisted on buying when we bought the townhouse together.

What girl wouldn't love her boyfriend in this state? When he got like this, he wanted one thing and one thing only. I could see him trying to be patient and wait for me to invite him closer to me, but he was fidgeting. Stretching luxuriously, I spread my legs just enough for him to catch a glimpse of my wet trim. Catching his breath, he looked as if he was trying very hard not to jump on me, which just got me hotter.

"Something you want, princess?"

"Please! Let me lick your pussy, Daddy. I want to so bad," he whispered urgently.

I couldn't help but tease him just a little bit more. Reaching between my legs, I played with myself until I was wet enough to make a small puddle. He watched, rapt, and I could tell he desperately wanted to come closer, to smell and taste me. I could see his member quickly stiffening. I stopped teasing him when I couldn't take it anymore.

"Anything for my little girl," I purred. Spreading my legs just wide enough for him to cozy up close to my muff, I started to get whatever the chick equivalent of blue balls was. My clit throbbed painfully. This was why I loved this man—once he was all wound up, he could lick my pussy for hours. Settling back on his legs, he licked around my hood piercing in slow, sexy, circular movements, darting his tongue against the barbell every so often. He knew that this would make me moan louder than I already was. I was panting so quickly that my head swam, so I tried to make myself take a few slow breaths. His hands snaked up to my breasts and started pinching my nipples in rhythm with the movement of his tongue. I grabbed the back of his head and ground my clit against his mouth. I could feel his rock-hard cock rubbing against my foot.

"You want Daddy to come in your mouth, don't you?" I gasped out. He moaned in agreement and I felt him get even harder. "I'm going to come so hard in your mouth, you little minx." I tightened my grip against the back of his head, forcing him to take the rhythm I wanted, giving him no choice but to comply. The muscles in my thighs tightened as the lightheaded feeling I always got before coming overtook me. Desperate to get off, I thrust my pussy against his mouth hard until I felt myself cascading into orgasm. I tried to think of the neighbors, but failed, screaming, "Fuck! Fuck! Yeah! Oh, my god! Yeah!"

Gasping for breath, I choked out a "Good girl," and pulled him up close to me to snuggle for a moment while I tried to compose myself. I petted him as he lay next to me, obediently quiet, waiting for me. After a minute, his hard cock was too much of a distraction for me to lie calmly next to him. I reached under the bed and pulled out my strap-on setup, tumbling out of bed to lace up. I loved the feel of the leather and O-rings against the flesh of my hips, and the way the straps framed my butt.

At first I hadn't been sure of the dildo part; it seemed awfully big to me to use on him. A girl, sure, but it seemed like asking a lot from a guy. I suggested a plug because I tried not to ask for anything that I wasn't willing to do myself and I was doubtful at best that I would be willing to put a full-sized rather thick dildo in my own ass. But he laughed and said that at least mine was curved and ribbed to hit the right spots, and vibrated, which was more than he could say about his ex-boyfriends.

I never got why boys were so full of themselves about having a dick until I started wearing one myself on occasion. There's a certain feeling of power that came with having a cock that I enjoyed immensely. Once I was rigged up I took a moment, as I always did, to puff up my chest and admire the awesomeness of my member. I stroked my cock a few times to reacquaint myself, to enjoy the smooth feel of it jutting up underneath my hand.

"Come here, princess." He curled over to the side of the bed I was standing next to. "Suck Daddy off." I gently thrust my shaft inside his mouth, getting off on watching him go down on me, faux cock or not. Shameless as he is, he made eye contact with me the whole time. My clit started to tingle again, watching his mouth diligently swirl up and down my shaft. I loved what a champ he was in the sack; he never bitched and moaned about doing double oral duty. Not bitching much in general, but especially not in the bedroom—*and* doing the dishes? That was the key to my heart and quim.

I slipped my little bullet vibrator between the harness and my clit and pulled my prick out of his eager mouth. He moved over on the bed to make room for me and I nestled back into my pillows, pulling him over to ride me. Reaching over to the bedside table, I lubed up my perpetually rock-hard shaft. I entered him, allowing him to gently ease his hot little ass down onto my big, thick phallus. Once I was completely inside him, I grabbed his hips and slowly swirled mine, pulling out of him and then thrusting slowly back inside.

I could see why guys got off on watching a chick on top of them. There is something about a partner riding you; it's not a position that leaves room for much abandon. Being on top requires some sexy showmanship and secretly, there was nothing he loved more than putting on a show. He had his head back and was panting for me to fuck him harder. I dug my finger-nails into the fleshy part I loved above his hip bones and started thrusting harder and harder. I loved the feeling of the stretching of muscles in my legs and ass that don't usually get used. It was exhilarating, being put through my paces and feeling exercised in a way I never did when we had more traditional sex. Tradi-tional sex is always a good time, don't get me wrong, but that's more for lovemaking. This was about flat-out fucking someone I loved; lust tinged with love, not the other way around. The little buzzing vibrator was busily doing its job, getting me closer and closer to getting off with every bump and vibration. I grabbed his pecs roughly, cupping them and pinching his nipples hard, concentrating as I plunged up into him.

"Do you want to come, princess?"

"Please, Daddy!"

"You've been a very good girl. You may." I watched him reach down to stroke his own throbbing member as I continued to penetrate him using sharp, quick little thrusts. I was unable to resist the buzzing of the vibrator and the sight of him on my cock, thrusting into him, so it wasn't long before I came again, even before he did. His breaths came in ragged little gasps as he jerked himself off on top of me, coming all over my breasts. I gave him a moment to pull himself together before I gently pulled out. After he caught his breath, I cuddled him next to me. I wriggled out of the harness and put it on the bedside table.

"Good date night, baby?" I asked, kissing the top of his head.

"You are a sex god," he said sleepily, reaching up to kiss me.

"No, you are!" I giggled.

Both equally satisfied, we snuggled into our nightly spooning position and fell asleep, me snoring louder than him.

TEPPANYAKI

Janine Ashbless

Wendy always overdoes it when we have visitors. It takes her two days to clean the house from top to bottom—and I mean everywhere, even the places no one will see. The upper faces of door lintels and of curtain rails, the insides of cupboards, the second oven that we don't even use most of the year. She wants everything to be spotless. Then she'll spend hours deciding what to wear, and styling her hair and plucking her eyebrows and applying serum and foundation and things I can't even guess at, until her face has the flawless sheen of airbrushed porcelain. She has to look perfect when the door opens to our guests.

It drives me crazy.

Don't get me wrong: I like a clean house. I appreciate all the hard work she puts in. And I think Wendy is beautiful, with or without makeup. Oh, do I ever. She has the most fantastic creamy skin that shows up the big red imprint of my hand on her ass just like a brand. She has curves that can't fail to grab my attention: ample breasts that jut under her low-cut T-shirts, a big round butt that sways bewitchingly when she walks, and a deep waist that accepts the snug grasp of my hands just so. She complains all the time that she needs to lose weight but I don't see it. She's fucking perfect. Her hair is straight and brown and unusually thick, and when I pull it she gasps and parts her full lips in an O that's all cock-shaped promise. Then her eyes look up at me, wide with expectation, moist with the knowledge of tears to come. She only has to catch my gaze the right way—leaning forward to display her pillowy cleavage; lips pouting in contrition for some sin that I don't know about yet, or perhaps no sin except the itch of her own need that shames her so, even as it exalts and inflames mine—and I'm snagged on the hook of lust.

Tonight she's twittering round the kitchen at the last minute, ramming dirty clothes into the washing machine like she's trying to punish it. "I've still got the last lot of laundry to put away," she worries.

"Why?" I ask, as I slice the steak into thin strips. The meat opens under the sharp blade like juicy petals. "It's not like Jason and Maria are going to be looking in our airing cupboard."

Wendy shoots me a glare like I don't understand something of blinding, self-evident importance. She's crazy. She drives me crazy.

She loves for everything to be perfect, and I long to take that perfection and besmirch it.

It's all that effort she puts in that makes me value the act of vandalism. I long to smear her immaculate lipstick all over her face and my cock. I love to see mascara tears streaked down her cheeks, to see the white canvas of her ass painted with welts and scratches. I want to tear her sheer black nylons and splash come across her costly silks. I want to muss her hair and fuck her until her dignity's torn to shreds and she's flushed and squealing and unable to contain herself, incoherent with the shock of orgasm after orgasm. It's the only way I can pay tribute to such immaculate beauty.

I'm just the kind of guy who likes to walk across fresh-fallen snow.

"I just want it to be right, so I can relax," she says.

"The place looks great. And you look amazing." If my hands weren't covered in meat juices I'd grab her, but at this stage she'd just rush off to get changed. I pretend to do so anyway and she shies away from me, flicking me with a tea towel.

"First impressions count, Ade."

"Oh, don't worry. First impressions are going to knock them out."

"Do you think they'll like teppanyaki?" This is the first time she's met my colleague or his wife.

"It's meat. Jason will like it." I go to wash my hands.

"Did you ask?"

"No."

"But what if they don't like Japanese food?"

"They'll love it. And if they don't, I'll tell the Chief Inspector about the photos Jason keeps on his laptop."

Wendy giggles, half irritated, half nervous.

I put my hands on her bare shoulders. She's wearing a sleeveless white *broderie anglaise* blouse, very tight all the way down to the hips where it flares out, and with buttons down the front. Beneath it, her skirt is bright red. I like her wearing skirts; at work everything and everyone is functional and masculine and drab. I like to come home and get my hands on something soft and feminine, all curves and color and yielding warmth. "It'll be great, Wendy. Now, are you ready?"

"I am, but..."

"Come on."

I steer her into the dining room where the table is laid for dinner. Pride of place goes to a round teppanyaki griddle where the food will be cooked. We've got little rectangular rice-porcelain plates and matching rice bowls in blue-and-white, a bottle of expensive sake warming in a water bath, three different bottles of soya sauce, fresh wasabi and pickled ginger. Tongs and chopsticks are the only cutlery. I've prepared all the food and it's waiting in the kitchen, the rice keeping warm in the electric steamer. Everything in the room is polished and gleaming.

"Okay, sit down for a minute, Wendy."

"I need to do the laundry—"

My hand goes to the hair at the back of her head, holding her firmly so she has to look me in the eye. When I do that, she knows she has to listen. I see her pupils darken. "Sit down," I say softly.

"Okay," she mumbles, only half submissive, sticking her lower lip out in a pout. But she sits on one of the dining chairs.

"You've got to relax, love. This is supposed to be my birthday treat. It's supposed to be fun."

"I know." She pulls a face. "It's just the way I am."

"Let me give you a neck rub and see if we can change that."

The chairs are straight backed and upholstered in dark leather. There are horizontal rungs up the backs that are meant to be decorative but which have certain practical possibilities I've been bearing in mind for some time. I stand behind her and start to knead her shoulders and up the nape of her neck into her scalp. She can never resist that. It takes a few moments before she yields to me, but I feel her tension ease and I reward her by expanding my repertoire, stroking her throat, tracing blunt nails over the smooth skin of her shoulders, lifting her jaw to draw her head back against my stomach.

"Shut your eyes," I murmur, but I hardly need to instruct her. I bet Wendy would make a fantastic subject for hypnotism: she responds so well to firm guidance. I reach down to stroke the skin of her décolletage with feathery gentleness, and she sighs. I see the first sign of her nipples starting to poke against the white cotton dress. It seems a shame not to give them the attention they yearn for and I stoop to flick and pluck those firm points, feeling them harden with naive eagerness. My cock surges too, furtively.

"Oh," she whispers.

"Relax, honey."

"Mm."

"You really do look beautiful, you know. I love that skirt; just short enough to tease."

She giggles and I feel the vibration in her throat against my fingers as I stroke her. Her throat is an incredibly vulnerable point for her. When she gets really aroused, close to orgasm, she likes me to grip it firmly, threatening to cut off her breath. She likes the fear.

Gently, I lift her arms, drawing them up over her head. It's a familiar relaxation move. She lets me pull the long muscles, not resisting as I straighten her spine. Releasing the tension, I lower one wrist back to her side. My hand goes in my trouser pocket without her realizing it. There's a clink, a touch of body-warmed metal, the sound of a tiny ratchet clicking home. A tremor runs through her and I'm guessing her eyes have opened again, puzzled.

I've snapped one bracelet of my regulation-issue handcuffs around her left wrist.

Before she has time to react, I make my move. Both hands down, behind her back. The chain through the rung of the chair. Both wrists captive.

"Ade?" she protests. "Have we got time for this?"

I pull the chair, and her on it, back from the table. "Open your legs," I tell her, crossing round to stand face-to-face.

She is bright eyed, uncertain; her lips are parted and moist. She would protest, but my caresses have undermined her resistance. Already her body's deep instincts are taking control, and when I look her in the eyes and repeat my command, she obeys.

"We've got time," I whisper, hunkering down and reaching between her parted thighs to the hidden gusset of her panties. "Wider."

She shifts a little to grant me access. I'm watching her face and I see the tip of her tongue appear against her teeth. That and the catch of her breath let me know I've found her clit beneath the fabric. I flick it with rapid movements, my nail making a tiny purring noise on the cloth.

"Oh, that's nice," she says.

"Shut up," I tell her softly, and I see the bloom of grateful warmth in her eyes. "Shut up and take it."

She leans back and half shuts her eyes, thrusting out her lovely tits. The cloth strains across the mass of her orbs, making my mouth water. Her hips tilt as I carry on flicking her switch, and the motion lifts her pussy up to my hand. Greedy girl. Always. And so responsive to the right words that it's almost dangerous. Her heat, so precariously hidden, is a constant provocation to me. Now she whimpers softly under her breath, finding the teasing of my finger both pleasurable and tormenting. She's starting to want more.

I decide to give her more. Tucking my finger under the elasticized edge of her panties, I slip my fingertips into the wet warmth contained within.

"Oh, you're wet," I tell her. She turns her face away against her shoulder, her breasts rising in sharp little heaves. "Do you like this, then? Do you like being tied up and made to open your legs so I can touch your pussy? Are you a *dirty* little girl?"

That's enough to make her moan. So I give her what she really wants and run my slippery fingertip all over the hot, stiff nubbin of her clit.

That's the moment the doorbell rings.

"Right on time," I say, withdrawing my hand and standing. "Jason's never late."

Wendy's face is a picture. Her thighs slap together. "Shit! Ade, let me out!"

I lift my fingers to my face, savoring the perfume of her pussy, and grin. "No, I don't think so."

Her eyes go round. "Ade!"

"What, honey? Are you worried I'm going to bring a work colleague and his wife in here? That they're going to see you tied to a chair, helpless, with your skirt all rucked up like that? That they're going to know your pussy is all juiced up and ready for it?"

Her makeup is perfect, of course, but I'm delighted to see an explosive flush of pink across her throat and chest and shoulders as the shame flares within her. She makes a valiant, if completely vain, attempt to smooth down her skirt by writhing her thighs, and then pulls forward, tugging against the handcuffs. "Ade!" she cries. "Stop it! You can't!"

Of course, Wendy should know—in fact she does know, when thinking straight—that the sight of her struggling against bonds just puts hot lead in my balls. "Can't?" I ask, rubbing one hand across the hard-on now making its urgent presence felt inside my pants.

"I don't even know these people!"

"That's funny. Because they're going to know a lot about you, very soon. About what a hot and dirty wife I've got."

"Please!"

Oh, that gets me harder than an iron bar. I step in, lift her chin in my hand and look into her wide eyes. Tears of terror are welling up there. "Want to beg me?" I whisper harshly.

"Please Ade! Oh, god, please! I can't—I can't do it! I'll die of shame! Please don't!"

I cock an eyebrow, waiting, my swollen cock pressing up against its own prison as vigorously as Wendy tugs against her cuffs. The first tear leaks over her lashes. She's utterly sincere: she means what she says and I don't doubt that she feels overwhelmed by humiliation.

But.

"What's the magic word?" I ask.

"Please! I'll do anything, Ade, but not this!" Her begging is heartbreakingly beautiful. Her eyes are like pools of torment and I want to fall into them.

"Will you beg me to fuck your ass?" Anal's a practice she retreats from, normally; it offends her overactive sense of cleanliness.

"Yes! Even that! Please!"

That isn't the magic word. I step back. "No," I say decisively. "I think I prefer this." Then I walk out. In the doorway I turn back and look at her, giving her one more chance. We have a safeword, of course. But Wendy's pulling wordlessly against the steel bonds, her lips parted as if in agony and her breasts heaving. Utterly fucking beautiful. And mute.

Jason and Maria are waiting patiently at the front door when I open it; I had warned them I might be a few minutes.

"Come in! Let me take those coats." I usher them into the hallway and kiss Maria on either cheek. Jason had told me she's Spanish, but this is the first time we've met. She has a sweet smile full of suppressed excitement and barely comes up to

Jason's breast pocket. He's all bone and paleness, his skin tight over his sharp cheekbones. She looks exquisite in a red dress. I think Wendy's going to like them both.

"We've been looking forward to this, Ade."

Jason and I have worked together a couple of times on different cases. He's sound: a rock-solid sort. You can learn a hell of a lot about a guy when you share long surveillance shifts with him.

"Well, we're all ready for you. Wendy's just through in the dining room."

Jason and Maria swing. Wendy and I don't, because I don't like the idea of some other man fucking my wife. She's mine. And Wendy knows I'm the possessive type and likes it that way; it makes her feel special. So we don't move in Jason and Maria's circles. But there are, I guess you'd say, areas where our interests as couples overlap.

As I lead the way back into the dining room, my heart lifts with pride at the picture presented. Wendy has ceased fighting the cuffs and is sitting up very straight with her feet tucked beneath the chair, trying to look as demure as it's possible to do with wrists tied. Her face is averted self-consciously, her lips parted and shiny.

Perfect.

"Maria, Jason, this is Wendy. She's feeling a bit shy at the moment, I'm afraid. Wendy, say hello."

"Hello," she whispers. "How lovely to meet you."

I know how difficult she must be finding this. How impossible it must be for her, in that hot swamp of her embarrassment, to find the right social chitchat. So I make things easy for her: "Wendy, you're to be silent now. Open your legs."

She eases her thighs apart. I could explode with pride. Jason is standing with his hands in his pockets, a big grin plastered all over his face. Maria goes forward and stoops, kissing her on the cheek.

"What a lovely outfit, Wendy," she murmurs. "Ade has told us so much about you."

I take our guests through to the kitchen to pour the first drinks and open the rice steamer and explain how teppanyaki works, but only one tiny part of my mind is on the small talk or the cooking. My hard-on is verging on the distressing. This is the first time I've allowed anyone else to admire Wendy so intimately and my physical reaction surprises even me.

We return to the dining table; Maria insists on helping me carry the food through. Before dinner begins, I push Wendy's skirt up her thighs to reveal the plump lace-covered mound of her sex, and hook a finger under her panty elastic. The kitchen scissors shear through the fabric without effort, and I drop the ruined underwear beneath the table. Her pussy is, of course, perfectly shaven—anything less would be too untidy for Wendy—and as I pat it softly, she twists and whimpers. I hear Jason chuckle and make some remark to his wife in a low voice.

Hooking a foot around the leg of Wendy's chair, I drag it closer to the table so she is within reach as I sit.

Dinner begins. Teppanyaki is a sociable, interactive way to eat. Lumps are plucked from the block of butter and dropped on the hot griddle, slicking the black metal plate. Then food is laid on with chopsticks to cook as we wait, each piece needing only a few minutes to fry, and replaced as soon as it's plucked by fresh morsels: steak slices and tuna and chicken, asparagus spears and mushrooms, crisp mange-tout pea pods and—defying tradition—white strips of halloumi cheese that brown without melting. The smell of hot butter and griddled meat is enticing. We dip the cooked food in tiny individual bowls of soya sauce stirred with hot green wasabi paste, and my lips tingle. We talk, inconsequentially, ignoring Wendy and her predicament, but each of us glancing at her often.

Of course Wendy can't feed herself. She is dependent on me to cook her food for her and offer it to her lips with my chopsticks. She seems a little reluctant to eat, preoccupied with her own woe, but she takes each piece obediently. It's not easy to be neat, either. The first time a drop of melted butter falls from a pea pod onto the white lawn of her dress, Maria pipes up, "Oh—you don't want to get oil on that, Ade. It'll never come out!"

I nod, standing, and go over behind Wendy. She realizes what I'm doing and the cuffs rattle as she jerks her arms, trying to stop me before she remembers that she has no chance. Shock dances in her eyes. "Please!" she squeals as I start on the little buttons over her jiggling breasts.

I grip her jaw, pulling her head back. She stares up in terror, her hazel eyes so dilated that they're almost black. "Shut up. What did I tell you, Wendy? You're to be quiet." And, magically, she goes still in my grasp, trembling a little but no longer fighting me. I undo her blouse buttons without any fuss, revealing a magenta bra that matches the panties I've already destroyed and the creamy slopes of her generous cleavage. Scooping her breasts from the lacy cups, I bare her to our guests.

"Wow!" says Jason, a cup of sake frozen halfway to his lips.

"Your wife has beautiful tits," Maria agrees, awestruck.

As she should be. Wendy's breasts are magnificent. I take her nipples between the finger and thumb of each hand and pull them out, encouraging the flesh to swell and harden.

"I'm thinking of having them pierced," I confide, as Wendy moans low in her throat.

"You should," says Jason. "Have you thought of having a chain strung between them?"

I smile darkly. I've thought of lots of things. With my open hands I slap her tits to make them bounce, one after the other. Jason shakes his head, grinning, and Maria mimes an "Ow!" and flashes her eyes. But Wendy only quivers.

Back to dinner, and from now on I make sure that the food I offer my wife is well soused in the hot butter. It drips generously upon her tits, dribbling down to grease her erect nipples. It's a little painful, of course, but Wendy is well used to that. She only jerks and moans a little with each splash, and her discipline in the face of suffering makes my blood race. What I really want is to see her self-control—that same self-control I enjoined upon her—crumble. But I get the most response when I take a stem of asparagus, brilliant green and glistening with warm butter, test its heat against my wrist and then inveigle it into the split of her plump sex before plucking it out again and inserting it, piquant with new sauce, into her mouth. Then she writhes with shame.

Despite all my culinary efforts, no one's mind is on the food now. When I follow up the asparagus by dabbing my fingertip in the wasabi and soya mix and painting it delicately over Wendy's clit, Jason sits back and adjusts the bulge at his crotch, his eyes bright and hard. "Oh, that's cruel," he says appreciatively.

Wendy's breath hisses between her clenched teeth as the burn starts. I take a thoughtful sip of my sake as she presses her thighs together, trying to relieve the sensation. There's a dew of sweat at the cusp of her throat and I want to taste it. Soon she's rubbing her thighs against each other, her tits quivering in a breathtaking manner as she wriggles.

"Is that hot, honey?" I ask.

Wendy doesn't speak, but she nods rapidly.

"Oh, please, Ade," says Maria suddenly. "Please let me lick it off her."

Now that takes me by surprise. I'd warned Jason there'd be

no hands-on stuff. But now, with my cock threatening to burst my fly and my balls practically blue, the thought of that pretty little woman lapping at my wife's pussy has distinct appeal. Maria has a pouting cocksucker mouth and her lips are parted eagerly as she awaits my permission. "Go on then," I say gruffly. Standing, I pull my wife's chair out a little. "Wendy, get your feet up on the table."

She lets slip a thrilling groan as she obeys, though whether this is further evidence of her humiliation or simply dismay at having to open her burning pussy, I don't know. She's wearing strappy red high heels to match her skirt. I stand behind her and tilt her chair back on its rear legs to make it easier to get her feet up on the table edge, admiring the view of her spread thighs and pointed toes.

Maria has to kneel to duck under Wendy's leg and get between her thighs. I like that; I can't help wondering if she'd kneel with such alacrity for me. Probably, yeah, I think. She has a round, eminently spankable bottom despite being such a forward little hussy—but that's a thought I put away for another day. Right now I've got more than enough to occupy my attention with what's going on, as she delicately parts Wendy's pussy lips with her fingers and tongues the flushed, pink split between.

God, that's a sight to remember for a lifetime: my wife with thighs spread wide and bare breasts upthrust, a dark head busy between her pale legs, her wrists tied mercilessly behind her. It's a sight Jason can't resist, either; he leaves his place and comes round to get a good look at his wife at work on mine. He's enough in command of himself to pull the electric flex on the griddle first, though—like I said, a sound guy. There's melted butter slicked all over the jiggling mounds of Wendy's tits and I want to smother my face in them. But it's my task to hold the chair so she can't fall, my task to watch as she bucks and slides to her first orgasm, forgetting the command to be silent as her squeals break free. She doesn't shut her eyes as she comes. She doesn't look down at Maria, or across at Jason. She has eyes for me only, staring up at me, transfixed and accusing, in full acknowledgment that I alone am the source of her degradation and her pleasure. I'm the only one who can take care of her in her extraordinary and humiliating need.

Maria doesn't stop. I'm impressed despite myself; she shows real dedication to eating out my wife. Because that's the thing about Wendy: once she gets started on oral she can come over and over again with only a few moments between, like a string of Chinese firecrackers. Six, nine, a dozen times, on occasion— until she's hysterical with exhaustion but still capable of being wrung out one more time.

I glance over at Jason as she shrieks again, grinding her pussy against Maria's mouth. He's standing very politely, one hand cupping his clothed crotch and an expression of concentration on his face as he watches. Something goes off in my head. A door never opened before.

"Wendy, honey," I say, "open your mouth for the nice man."

We don't swing. I don't let my wife fuck around with other guys. But the notion of being able to *give her away at my whim*—and to someone she's never met before—that lights a fire in my balls.

"Oh!" she cries, half protesting.

I grip her jaw. "Open."

So Jason steps in, unzipping, catching his cock as it bounces out and angling it toward my wife's open mouth. I tilt the chair to present her at the easiest angle. It's a veiny dick, still pale despite being engorged. When Wendy takes it in all the way, gobbling it eagerly down, I feel a rush of pride. She's just so good.

Then he fucks her mouth, rather more gently than is my own habit, while his wife lashes Wendy's clit until my beautiful, horny little slut comes again. And again. Her cries are muffled this time though, by all that cock down her throat. She bucks eloquently instead.

I feel like a god. Lord of all I survey.

"Okay," huffs Jason, eyes slitted. "What should...?"

"Mess up her tits," I say. I sound calm, though my racing blood could fuel rockets right now. Jason obeys me, too: he pulls out and directs his cock over her chest, and with a few tugs he pumps his load in great splashes all over Wendy's big tits. The sight is branded on my inner vision forever. Wendy's sobs of shame are like music.

Maria lifts her head, grinning.

Jason's little grunt of release is followed by a long sigh of satisfaction.

"Come on," says Maria, wriggling out from under Wendy's legs. "Time for us to go home, I think." She catches what must be my look of surprise. "Twenty minutes home," she explains, "and then he'll go *all night* on the strength of that. And you don't need us around, Ade."

I don't argue. I do see them to the door; it's only polite, after all. By the time I make it back, Wendy has caught her breath and is upright, sagging forward a little against her bonds. Her breasts glisten.

"They said 'Thank you for a lovely evening,'" I tell her.

She looks up at me, her eyes round. She's smeared with butter and jizz and sweat. Her makeup is running.

"You," I grunt, unlocking the cuffs and hoisting her to her feet, "were the perfect hostess." I relock the steel bracelet so that her arms are still caught behind her, only now free of the chair. It gives me the opportunity to push her facedown onto the table. Crockery clatters and cups spill, but I ignore them. I think she has one breast squashed into a plate of soya sauce. "You were the good time had by all," I continue, slapping her asscheek good and hard. Wendy gasps, her senses not entirely numbed yet. I even up the slaps by swatting her other buttock, just in the interest of fairness. Then, pinning her over the table with one hand, I reach with the other to the block of butter. It's softened while sitting near the hot griddle into a yellow, slippery cream. "Look at you," I chide, sliding my fingers and a great oozing gobbet of butter between her asscheeks. "Look what a fucking mess you are. You dirty...fucking...girl."

The clench of her anus offers no resistance to my fingers. I lube her up well, plunging two broad digits into her as deep as they'll go, enjoying her whimpers.

"What have you got to say for yourself?" I ask, as I poise my cockhead at her back entrance, its blunt bell end threatening the ultimate humiliation.

"Please Ade," she moans. "Please fuck my ass!"

"Like this?" I push in, slow and hard.

"Yes! Oh, fuck yes!"

I've been feeling like a loaded gun all evening. Now the safety catch is off. "You dirty girl," I groan, just before I lose the power of speech altogether. "You dirty, dirty girl." Then I'm shafting her buttery depths, ramming up to the hilt, spreading her cheeks with my hands so that on the backstroke I can see my cock impaling her great big beautiful ass.

Hearing her come, one more time.

Just before I do, too. In my dirty, beautiful, wonderful wife.

GREASING THE WHEELS

Madlyn March

My hands felt shaky as they typed on his computer. I looked back to make sure he wasn't coming. I took a lucky guess at his password.

And then I found it. I actually found it.

Thanks for last night. Love, Debbie.

It was an email that proved what I'd long suspected: my boyfriend was cheating on me. I felt—well, obviously anger, but also relief. So I wasn't crazy, after all.

The email came with an attachment. It was a photo of Mark wearing women's underwear, and Debbie was by his side, kitten with a whip.

I couldn't believe it. Of all the men I'd dated, Mark seemed the most conservative. Last time we were together, I had lightly patted his ass, and he got super freaked out, saying he wasn't into any of that weird stuff.

Well, it doesn't get any weirder than a hairy dude dressed in some frilly lingerie with all his appendages attached to a chair.

I looked at the photo again. She was blonde, blue-eyed and busty—just the kind of woman you'd expect your boyfriend to cheat on you with. As for Mark, his face looked like he was in a tremendous amount of pain and yet his cock was enormous.

I know, I know: it was wrong of me to get turned on by such a creep, but I couldn't help myself.

Now, what was I going to do about it?

Out of the corner of my eye, I saw a candlestick. Mark had gone into the bathroom just five minutes ago, so I was sure I still had plenty of time. It was a little difficult slipping the candlestick in me because I wasn't very wet yet, but it eventually reached its destination. I lay there for a few moments, enjoying the feeling of being filled by something so huge. I gently stroked my swelling nub and pinched my hard nipples. And then, just as I was about to get down to some real fucking, Mark flushed the toilet.

"Shit!" I yelled. I massaged my clit some more, hoping to eke out some kind of fast orgasm, but it didn't work. I tried to get the candlestick out; it wouldn't budge. Lord, I'd die if I had to explain this to some emergency room doctor.

I pulled up my panties. I didn't know how I was going to have a normal conversation with what felt like John Holmes's dick inside of me, but I was going to have to try.

Mark came out of the bathroom, talking about how he was now a full ten pounds lighter.

"Where's my candlestick?" he asked.

"What?"

"My mother's candlestick. It's always here, right on the coffee table." He crouched down to look under the table.

"Oh, yeah, well, that," I said, casually. "Yeah, well, you see. It's, um, up my crotch."

He got up off the floor and his eyes slowly grew wide. "What?

What the hell is it doing there?"

Being used in a new type of menorah, I almost answered, but then thought better.

"I was, um, masturbating," I said, my face reddening.

"You were *what?*"

"Listen, you've got to help me!" I said, shaking him. "I can't get it out!"

"All right, all right. Calm down. Let me see."

I opened my legs. He stared at my cooch, like a plumber would at a leaky sink. "Wow. You really jammed that thing up there, didn't you?"

He bent down and tried to pull it out, but it still wouldn't come loose. "I think the problem is that you're too dry. Is there anything I could do to, you know, uh, grease the wheels, as they might say?"

Part of me was excited by this suggestion, but the other part was sad, as I realized it took a major medical crisis for my boyfriend to ask what I wanted sexually. "Well, this is probably a strange thing to request, but would you mind wearing my underwear?"

He looked down at the floor, obviously fearful that I would see the excitement spreading on his face. "Oh," he said. "That turns you on? Well, sure. I guess I can. I mean, if it'll help."

I couldn't believe him. What was the big deal, admitting he liked wearing women's panties? I handed him my underwear and sat on the edge of the couch while he changed. I took a quick gander around the room and noticed the whip hanging in a closet. He was still struggling, trying to fit in my panties, so he didn't see me grab it. As he stood up, I smacked his ass with it, hard.

"What the—?"

"Oh, don't play coy with me," I said. "I know you like it

rough. I saw your little photo with Debbie there, you big cheater."

"You went through my emails?"

"Well, what was I supposed to do? I had a feeling something was up. Just didn't know it was your dick in another woman."

"Shit," he said. "Look, Megan, I've been under a lot of stress." I put a hand up. "Save your breath. I don't care."

"You don't?"

"No. Because after tonight, I'm through with you."

"Oh, Megan, no, please. I love you." He reached for me, in an attempt to give me a hug, but I pushed him away so hard he fell on the floor.

"Don't," I warned.

He folded his arms. "Okay. If that's the way you want it. But I really hope you'll reconsider, maybe in a few—"

"Listen to me," I said, pulling on his hair. "I'm not reconsidering anything, you fucking jackass. You don't deserve to have me as a girlfriend. You don't deserve to have any woman as your girlfriend. So let's just get this out of the way so I can get this fucking candlestick out of me, okay?"

I walked over to one of his chairs and told him to lie on my lap. "Lucky for you, I like to top just as much as you like to bottom. Not that you ever would have thought to ask me about it. Not that you ever would have thought to ask me anything about what I wanted in this relationship. But that's ancient history; now, on to the present. I want to let you know that while I enjoy topping a man, I don't enjoy causing him permanent bodily harm, so you can tell me to stop this at any time and I will. Understood?"

He nodded and I needed no further encouragement. I smacked his ass with the whip, hard. He shrieked and red welts formed almost instantly on his firm, pale buttocks. Soon,

Mark's tears began to moisten my skirt, his fingernails dug deep into my thighs and his breathing became labored, but he did not tell me to stop.

I was impressed.

His erection poked at my thigh. I whipped him extra hard when I discovered that, telling him he had no right getting excited before I allowed it.

"Tell me something," I asked. "When's the last time you went to the doctor?"

"What? I, uh, don't remember."

"Well," I said, "I think you're due for a thorough rectal examination, don't you?" I pulled down his panties and stuck a long finger into his tight little hole.

He groaned. I pulled my finger out. "I can't believe you! This is a professional doctor's exam and here you are, getting excited by it. What kind of sick fuck are you? We'll have to train you out of that disgusting habit," I said, as I began whipping him again. "Although I know it's hard. To tell you the truth, I'm getting a little excited right now myself, Mark. You can't see me, but I'm fondling my tits and playing with my clit and ooooohhh, I'm getting so excited."

"Please," he said.

"Please what?" I asked.

"Please blow me."

I smacked his head.

"I mean, please, Mistress."

"Better."

I told him to sit on the couch. He winced as his ass touched the cushion. Slowly, I took his silk panties down and blew him, my warm mouth covering his manhood as his hands gently guided my head.

His eyes rolled back and he moaned. And then, with a quick

jerk of his hips, he exploded inside my mouth, unleashing an hour's worth of pent-up sexual frustration and what felt like almost a gallon of come. His entire body relaxed; he reminded me of a deflated balloon. I played with my clit while he was recovering.

"So, you want me to fuck you with the candlestick now?" he asked.

"Maybe later. Right now you can eat me out."

He backed away from me like I was made of something radioactive. "Uh, I'm not too good with that."

"You mean you don't like eating pussy."

"Well, it's not that so much. More like I feel I wouldn't be any good at it. Wouldn't you rather get fucked by the candlestick, anyway? I mean, that seems like it would be a lot more fun. And then maybe you could, you know, punish me, again."

"Listen," I said, grabbing him by the hair. "You will inhale my cunt or I'm leaving right now."

"Ow. Okay, okay."

He stared at my cunt for a few moments, as though he'd never seen one. I felt like he was mentally preparing himself for the task, the way David Blaine might before completing one of his death-defying stunts.

"Here," I said. "Let me help you." And then I pushed his face in between my legs.

He tried to get into the rhythm of going down on me, but he was too slow; for me it was like waiting for the train when I needed to get home yesterday. "You're right. You're terrible," I said. "Look. Why don't you just pretend it's a blazing summer's day and I'm a melting ice-cream cone. Wouldn't want any of it to drip, now would you?"

I lay back again and closed my eyes, as his tongue licked at a faster pace. He then got the bright idea of taking my clit between his lips and sucking it deep into his mouth.

I thought I would pass out.

He stopped to catch his breath, sighing for a minute, and I groaned as his soft breath tickled my pubic hair.

It was time.

"Go on, then," I said. "Fuck me."

Carefully, he removed the long stick from my hole, and then, not so carefully, he plunged it all the way back in. I felt like I was being split in two.

"Oh, god, Mark. It hurts."

"Does it?" he asked. "Well, I can stop. But if I do, I'll just have to leave you like this—horny and with a huge stick up your cunt for hours."

I couldn't believe him. He was trying to top me. I was so mad I felt like leaving, but my cunt wouldn't let me.

"All right," I said, "but try to be care—uuggh," I cried, as he pulled it out and shoved it in again. The pain was almost unbearable, but he pushed on my clit firmly with a finger, and that helped take my mind off things.

"You like that?" he asked.

"Yes."

"Well, to get more, you'll have to suffer," he said, giving me another painful fuck with the candlestick. Now, I was the one who was crying.

He licked my tears. "There, there, sweet Megan. This will all be over soon."

He climbed on top of me and took a breast into his mouth. He began sucking on the nipple, then biting down on it hard. I screamed. I looked down at my pussy and saw that I was gushing profusely.

That was the moment I became a convert—a convert to the life of the bottom.

Finally, he took the stick out for good and walked me over to the bathroom. Once we were there, he pushed me up against the sink and shoved his dick in my ass. I screamed as I was being impaled.

"You fucking bitch," he said, putting a hand over my mouth. "Do you want the whole neighborhood to hear?"

He reached around my waist to finger my clit. I struggled to stand as waves of pleasure turned my thighs into Jell-O. Another finger pushed into my hole and I felt the first wave of orgasm trying to burst out of me, but then he removed his hand.

"Now lie down," he ordered.

I tried to reach down to touch myself, but he held my wrists behind my back.

"Lie down," he repeated.

I stretched out on the pink shag carpet and he lay by my side. He stuck a finger in my hole, and then another, and then another, and soon I realized I was about to be fisted. My cunt swallowed his hand like it was starving.

"Now you'll come," he said, as he pressed deeply into my hole and thumbed my clit. And he was right; I came—sobbing, screaming, my whole body quaking.

"Meg?" he asked.

"What?"

"Maybe you could—"

"No, Mark. I can't. I mean, this was fun and all but I can't go out with you again. I can't forgive you for cheating on me."

"I know. That's not what I was going to say. What I was going to suggest is you come over next Monday and I'll leave that candlestick out on the table for you."

"Well, I—I—I'd have to think about that." Actually, I knew my answer. But *Let him suffer*, I thought. *Let him suffer.*

INTERVIEW

Talon Rihai and Salome Wilde

No, don't laugh. I didn't mean it like that. It's what Mistress wants that gives me what I want, you know? It's not that asking my permission for this interview is silly—I could say no, I suppose, if I wanted to. I'd need to have a damn good reason and be ready for Mistress to punish me or worse. Mistress invited you into her home to conduct this interview and that's all I need to know. Well, that and my being thrilled with this opportunity to share just how amazing it is to be hers.

So, your first question is "Why Mei?" That's easy. Or, anyway, I'm totally clear on the answer. Mei is my Mistress because she claimed that role in my life. She claimed it before I even knew I wanted a Mistress. Well, maybe that's not quite right. I knew I wanted something, or someone, to help me find myself. Do you know what I mean? Not a shrink or anything like that. Not a parent or a wife. Okay, I guess it's not as simple as I thought. Let me put it this way: I'm a big, strong guy, the independent type, a loner. Everyone assumes guys like me are strong in personality, too. Dominant, macho, like that. But I'm not. I can take care of myself, sure, and I do. Dropped out of school and left home and found a job with a roofing company and stayed with it until I had a real solid career going, could afford even to buy my own house and feel proud of myself. But with people? I'm shy, I guess. Don't like to make the first move. Don't really have friends other than the guys I work with. Never dated much.

Mistress—Mei—is the one who approached me, but you could guess that. Saw me on the roof next door to her place and yelled something up to me I couldn't quite hear. I thought it must be important, so I made the "one minute" sign, finished what I was doing and came down. Turns out she was just saying it was a nice day...and that I looked good in a tank top. I just stood there. That floored me. I'm not ugly, I don't think, but I don't get a lot of compliments. Or if I get them, I don't recognize them as compliments. That's what Mistress thinks. Anyhow, I was all sweaty and must've been blushing right up to my eyebrows. She told me to come into her house. The other guys were working and either didn't notice or pretended not to, so I went in. There was something in how she said it. Not inviting: telling. And something in me responded. Hard. She was half my size, older than me, pretty. Not all made-up or being seductive like bad porn. She was dressed real casual. But she had this way about her. Like she knew what I needed, and if I only went into her house and did what she said, I'd find it. Find happiness. Sounds stupid when I say it like that. But it's true. She knew—she knows. From that first day, she was my Mistress.

Ah, my turn, is it? Such a sweet tribute from my boy. I don't think I've heard Harry say so much since the first day we met. And I would love to tell you about that day. I was between play-toys at the time, my last one having been a particularly high-spirited, ginger-haired young lady. Firm body, firm breasts and ass and beautiful when she submitted. I do like a spirited sub. But there's spirited and there's insubordinate, and so we'd parted company. For days afterward, I'd been working from home, listening to the banging going on next door. And one roofer in particular kept catching my eye—especially when I kept peeking out the windows at him. He was easily bigger and broader than the others and focused entirely on what he was doing at the time. Even from a distance, I could see that. His musculature was solid and though he looked clumsy, he wasn't. I watched him for two days before I called out to him. Testing him. I watched the way he moved to my voice, and the way his eyes followed me. When the door closed behind him, before I'd even touched him, I knew I'd never let him go. From that day on, Harry belonged to me.

I love sleeping at the foot of Mistress's bed. I think that answers the question, doesn't it? It's not about Mistress herself, I guess, but it says more than "I love how she dominates me," right? It's not that she wouldn't let me sleep next to her, and it's not like we never ever do that kind of traditional couple thing. But Mei keeps things separate: the mundane world, and then our world. And sleeping at the foot of her bed really does it for me. I've never fit right on beds, and now there's a reason to it. I'm curled up and not fitting but determined to sleep at her feet, you know? I could talk about how I love when she spanks and paddles me until I cry or how she ties me up and rides my cock and forbids me from coming until after she comes or not at all. And maybe Mistress would think I would name that kind of thing as my favorite thing, but I doubt it. I think she knows how I tick better than anyone else, ever. Better than I know myself, you could say.

* * *

Best of all, I love how Harry has devoted himself, his entire self, to me. To my pleasure. His single-minded focus is one of his best attributes and something my other subs have lacked in the past. Should we do some everyday task, such as shopping, for example, together, Harry fetches and carries and opens doors and serves me unobtrusively—sometimes, I think, without even being aware of what he's doing. My other subs were devoted, yes, but often my pleasure or displeasure was not the focal point of their lives, not truly. Harry is different. He has found his place, his calling, if you will. He belongs to me in every way. Can you possibly understand the level of utter subservience it takes to give oneself to another completely? Of course, there is sex and play and spankings. But there are also hours spent rubbing my feet, and nights spent sleeping at the foot of my bed. All that and more. I confess I never thought my perfect sub would be such a person. But he is.

Limits? No. No way. None. There's nothing I won't do. And I mean that. It goes deep, really deep. You could say, "Oh, but you wouldn't let her stab you," or something. But the truth is, yeah, I would. It's because I know that no way would she ever really put me in real danger. There's a big difference between dominance and just treating someone like crap, you know? It sounds stupid to say it like that, but I've seen stuff, mostly online, about how some guy tells his sub to shove a hairbrush up her ass or heat up a spoon on the stove and burn herself—and she does it. Like that proves devotion. Okay, so maybe, in a way, it does. But what does it prove about the Dom? Mistress told me to think about that, and I do. Funny how the more I give myself over to her, the more I think about things. I thought it would be the opposite: total submission, total passiveness. But it's not like that, not at all. Not just in doing things for her—like washing dishes or the more fun stuff like bathing her—that stuff is active, obviously. But in how I see myself, our relationship, the dynamics of dominance and submission, Mistress would say. The dynamics are more complicated and more simple than I thought. And more fulfilling than I dreamed.

Limits? Of course I have limits. Far too many Dominants out there don't seem to know the difference between dominance and bullying. Could I make him do anything I said, anything I wished? Of course I could. And I expect him to obey me. But I have to set limits for myself, and by doing so, of course set limits for my boy. After all, it isn't my job to just boss him around, don't you see? He has given himself to me, entirely. And that makes it my responsibility to take care of him, in all ways. To make sure he's safe and happy. How could he please me if he were not happy in my service? How could he bend over to take my hand up his ass if he did not feel entirely safe in my ability to look after his best interests? Knowing how to be a good Dom means understanding what it means to be a good sub. Of course I push his limits. That pleases us both. But I would never allow harm to come to him, by my hand, by his or by someone else's.

Ah yes, most memorable moment. Well, I knew that question was coming, so I've been thinking about it all along. Thinking about how other people might answer it. I don't want to not answer it; I'm not avoiding it. It's more like...can you pick one slap or one kiss or one word and say it was the best or most important between two people, between a Mistress and her boy? It feels disloyal, somehow. Or like it's reducing everything down to one thing and what we are, what I am for Mistress and what she is for me—it just can't be boiled down like that. It was hard enough to just say one thing I really love about her, about us. But anyhow, I knew this was coming, so I'll try. And I have a feeling this time that Mistress will pick the same moment. It involves me crying, okay, so first let's just get that right out there because it's such a stereotype, such a cliché, isn't it? The big burly dude crying at his Mistress's feet. And yeah, from the outside, that's what it was. That's what my most memorable "moment" is. But that's not what it really is, what it means to Mistress and me. The crying is part of what brought me there, but Mistress brought me to the crying. Can Mistress tell that part? Please, Mistress?

With my boy asking so nicely, I'm inclined to indulge him. It is always fascinating what brings a person to any sort of insightful moment, and while I can often predict what will touch off a sub's reactions, sometimes I am delightfully surprised.

It began simply enough: Harry worshipping my body at my bidding. He used to keep his hair quite short, for his work, but I made him grow it out so that I would have something to grip when I needed to guide his head. Also, because I enjoy pulling his hair. I had just allowed him to move up my legs from my toes. Part of what I was doing was building his endurance, his staying power; the other part was entirely for my pleasure. He was hard, so very hard and unable to climax, due in part to the cock-and-ball straps, but also my order. I moved his head slowly up the insides of my thighs, occasionally bringing his face up to taste my wetness, but only a taste before putting his tongue back to work on my thighs. I love to have my boy kneeling between my legs. I recall letting him have another taste and he took more than he had been permitted. Instead of jerking his head back and making him look up at me, I watched, as though impassive, as he dove between my legs, his arms bound behind him, his ankles shackled to the spacer and his ass just barely dusted with a faint rose color. I warned him, once, that if he did not stop, I would be very displeased, but I could tell he was too far gone to properly hear and obey me. And that simply would not do. And so I stood up, toppling him over as his hands and legs were bound in such a way that he could not stop his own fall and pinched his bare balls with my bare toes. That got his attention. It took another few moments before realization dawned on his face, in his eyes, and I knew he understood just how severe his transgression was.

Before he could begin to stammer for forgiveness, I knelt down to gag him, the broad leather gag with the thick but short rubber cock attachment buckled behind his head. I'd had it made just for him. I moved him so he knelt once again, then pushed him down until his chest rested on the floor. And I simply bid him to remain there until I returned, to think about what he had done and why he had done it and what I should do with such an undisciplined slave. Yes, I do call him a slave, when it suits me. But he is also my boy, my precious Harry. "Slave" reminds him, though, that his life, by his choice, is not his to command any longer. And now, my slave can tell you how it is that the incident affected him so as to end up at my feet, crying.

In the big picture of life, or even in our relationship overall, I'm thinking the actual act of disobedience might seem small. I wanted Mistress to describe it because she gets the context across. Even now, having heard her explain it, I could cry, but I can't imagine anyone else who isn't into this really getting why this is the moment I picked for us. For one, I'm not someone who rebels for the sake of rebellion. But there was definitely what Mistress calls a "transgression." I wanted more, and I just took it. I can't tell you how bad I feel about that, especially with that word, "transgression." That formal way with language Mistress has that just wraps me up and carries me away, like everything she does. I deserved punishment, and I knew it, and it just killed me that I'd disappointed her. I work really hard never to disappoint, let alone disobey. I felt utterly destroyed when she walked away. Can you understand that?

But it was also about how Mistress punished me then. I think people who aren't in this kind of relationship think punishment is all about spanking or beating—but that's reward, or it's play, not punishment. Refusal, denial: that's how Mistress punishes me. So, even though I was bound and gagged and that might totally turn me on like crazy another time, this time it was about isolating me, leaving me there in bondage but not serving like I wanted to, with my mouth full but not full of Mistress. It forced me to really feel what it meant to do wrong, to transgress, to fail someone I want to please with every fiber of my being. And I was uncomfortable as hell and crying my eyes out and this sense of shame just washed over me, through me, like a huge wave that took me under. Something inside just broke, and I felt like there was nothing left, no ego to protect, no performance to give. I was at absolute zero, but the weird thing was that it wasn't like hopeless depression. It was overwhelming shame that made me even more resolved to devote myself fully to Mistress, even more fully than I had. She had given me the gift of hitting bottom, if that makes sense, and I felt completely emptied and ready to be filled by serving Mei, my one true, perfect Mistress. I stopped my sobbing, quieted my mind and just waited for Mistress to return, hoping she would give me another chance, and determined to be everything and anything she expected of me, from that moment on.

* * *

Advice for the curious, eh? I suppose I could give you a rundown of safety and the general rules of the lifestyle, but you can find that anywhere. My advice to those who would be Doms is short and sweet: be a sub first. Even if, like me, you don't have a submissive cell in your body, be a sub first. I didn't fall into this lifestyle by accident or gradually; it was something I craved. And so I joined in the local and online BDSM community and took part as a top in my share of floggings and public humiliations. I enjoyed it, I was good at it, but something was missing. And it came to me only after I noticed differences within couples, in pairs or groups. The difference was in the sub, but the sub follows the Dom. So I had to ask what was different about the Dom. I thought maybe it wasn't something that could be taught. But I wasn't satisfied with that dead-end answer. After some soul searching, driven by a big dose of hunger for what I was missing, I decided to sub. Not casually and not publicly and not with just anyone. I went to a man who is still one of my best friends. Harry knows him well: Master Liam. But he didn't know that I served as Liam's submissive...until now.

I thought it would take a week tops for me to understand what I needed. What actually happened was that it took me a week just to realize I was focusing on the wrong things. I trusted Liam and felt he respected me, otherwise I wouldn't have done what I did, which was to ask him for one hour per day to not be his sub so I could ask questions about what he was doing and why; so I could be a better Dom. He refused me. And it took that rejection and a lot longer than a week for me to understand the significance of my request and his response. Long story short, I was his sub not for a week but for six months. It wasn't easy. But from the moment I agreed to his terms, from the moment I stopped thinking about how to get what I wanted and instead took what he gave—and demanded—I began to learn, really learn. I felt him question and test me, build me up and tear me down, over and over, and I realized how fully and deeply he owned his power. And that was what I had been missing and have been building within myself and in my relationships ever since. Harry is my perfect submissive because he is an achievement, the product of all my learning and growing. And I don't think I would be who I am or he would be who he is to me if I hadn't ever learned to sub.

I know you want an answer about our future to wrap up the interview, but I've got to be honest: I'm reeling from Mistress's admission that she submitted to Master Liam. To anyone, really. It's mind-blowing. And if I didn't already feel entirely beholden to her for what she's given me, the way she lets me know myself, know submission and how much it moves me, I would feel it now. Mistress already gives so much of herself, and now I find out she's given even more. I know people think the Dom is just giving orders, giving punishment, getting service. But it's so much more than that. I hope Mistress doesn't find me too bold in saying this, but no matter what I'm doing for her—oiling and massaging her beautiful body or scrubbing her bathtub in nothing but an apron—Mistress chooses my tasks perfectly. She knows what I need and she gives it to me. Pleasure or pain, sex or housework: I feel every moment we're together how truly she cares. And I can't hope for anything more or better, now and for as long as Mistress will keep me.

Prettily said, my Harry, and I'm honored by your devotion. That's what it's all about, in the end, like even the most vanilla of relationships—but a hell of a lot more fun. Harry and I

*complement each other, fill each other's deepest needs. Where
I see us in the future is right here. Whatever else life may bring
us, I can't think of any greater pleasure than keeping my boy at
the foot of my bed for the rest of our lives.*

I TEND TO HER

Justine Elyot

I hate it when she's ill.

Of course, I try not to show it. She's all too ready to assume that I view her malaise as an encumbrance or inconvenience; hard as I have worked on erasing it, she still clings to some of the old self-doubt and insecurity. What she doesn't realize is that my reasons for hating her illness have nothing to do with the concerts or dinner engagements I'll have to cancel on her behalf, nor the endless invalid fare I have to prepare. It's not even about the disorder in my perfectly listed and filed existence. It's the sheer effrontery of those fucking germs, doing to her what *I* should be doing. If her cheeks are flushed and her eyes moist, it should be me doing the flushing and moistening. I might like inflicting pain on her, but pain that is not of my making is fundamentally wrong.

So when Loveday arrived home one rainy night looking as if she had just returned from a rendezvous with a lover and sounding as if she'd swallowed chalk, my heart sank. That feverish hue and brilliance of eye should come after a good session with my strap, not a dull commute in the rain.

I set aside the slow movement of the horn concerto I was writing and felt her forehead: ridiculously hot.

"You're feverish," I diagnosed. "Get to bed. Now."

Words I had often uttered under happier circumstances, but this time they could lead to nothing interesting. Doctor and patient is a game we sometimes play—I actually have a real stethoscope, but I only know how to misuse it. There would be no invasive examination scene that night, and the thermometer I selected to take her temperature was not the one we usually used in the bedroom. I made her some honey and lemon with a tot of brandy and prepared an appropriately sympathetic manner.

"What have you been doing to yourself?" I asked her, handing over the glass.

"Nothing!" she croaked. "Germs don't care what you do. If they're out to get you, they will."

"Are you sure you weren't flirting with them?"

I gestured for her to open her mouth and slid the thermometer under that pink little tongue, the tongue that tickled and suckled and dug into my mouth, now neutralized by bastard bacteria.

"Because if I thought you were giving those streptococci the come-hither, Loveday, I would be most displeased," I continued. "And you know what happens when I'm displeased, don't you?"

Tough love is a concept I have a lot of time for.

My poor patient nodded, rendered mute by the thermometer. I suppose she knew it was an empty threat, intended to convey my sadness at her feeling ill, rather than actual wrath, but even at the height of her fever, the deployment of the D/s dynamic seemed to perk her up a little.

The news from the mercury was not good.

"I think you're officially ill," I said. "We'll have to add my current displeasure to your account. I'm going to give you three days, Loveday. For every day beyond that that you are coughing or sniffing or spending for the most part asleep, there will be a penalty."

"That's not fair," she moaned in a touchingly wobbly voice. I tutted and stroked her burning hands.

"When have I ever been fair?"

She knew better than to answer.

"So you'll need to make sure you get well as soon as possible, won't you?" I whispered. "No getting out of bed without permission. No trying to talk when your voice isn't ready. No disobeying Dr. Rossington's orders."

"No fun," she mouthed, pouting, and I tapped her hands in light reproof.

"Not until you're better. Now get some sleep."

I didn't want her to think that I was worried, and I wasn't really—it was a simple enough case of strep throat, to be treated with antibiotics, rest and care. But even though her confinement to bed meant I wrote three times as much of the concerto as I would have done otherwise, I couldn't completely ignore the tiny fear that she might never recover. That this might be it, and I might lose my Loveday. I rarely indulge myself in unbearable thoughts, but three o'clock in the morning brought them out with their pitchforks and snarling teeth while Loveday tossed and turned beside me.

I control fear with control.

I caught her visiting the bathroom without permission and it gave me a chance to connect with her as her master rather than her nurse, so I seized it, steering her back to the bed once she emerged.

"Since you can't be trusted to do as you're told," I said, "perhaps I need to tie you to the bed. Hmm? Should I?"

"No," she whispered. "I'll ask next time."

"You've got your phone. If I'm in another room, just send me a message."

"I will."

She looked so pitifully small and unfocused, lost in the blankets, that the image of her bound wrists that had drifted pleasantly to mind dissolved quickly.

I went back to the concerto.

On the third day, she rose again—well, not quite, but almost.

My phone trilled and I opened the text message from Loveday.

I need a doctor.

It felt like a blow to the stomach. She was taking a turn for the worse. Now what would I do?

I rushed to the bedroom, finding her bundled in the blankets but looking no worse than she had done earlier.

"Are you all right, Love? Why do you need a doctor? Are you feeling worse?"

She shook her head.

"I meant you," she warbled. "I need Doctor Rossington."

Did she mean…? I narrowed my eyes.

"You mean you just worried me on a whim?"

"I didn't mean to. I just felt the urgent need for some medical attention."

Her voice was still harsh and miles out of its normal register, but the seductive tone was hard to miss. Minx. Lying there in that grannyish nightgown with her blonde hair all over the place and those lush lips cracked and dry, she looked more gorgeous than I had ever seen her.

I moved to the foot of the bed and folded my arms.

"Medical attention? Well, I think I can provide that. Take off your nightgown."

She began pulling the capacious cotton thing over her head while I headed to the kitchen to prepare a basin of soapy water and a sponge.

When I brought it back in, she was naked on the bed with the blankets tossed aside, her breasts rising and falling fast, her eyes bright and her thighs clamped together. Ready for her treatment.

I didn't bother with the white coat, but I thought the rubber sheeting would probably come in handy, so I dragged it out from under the bed and unrolled it, making her lie on her back on top of it.

"Let's start with a bed bath, shall we?"

I rolled up my sleeves and took the sponge, lifting it high above her, looking forward to the first shocking splash on her breasts.

The drop fell and she veered to the side, her mouth opening to emit a squeal that couldn't come out. She needed more training. I had time to give it to her.

"Don't move," I ordered. "Or I'll tie you down. Keep perfectly still."

The sight of her fighting her natural impulses to squirm or shield her defenseless breasts as the drops fell, flowing from her stiffening nipples down the slopes they perched upon, was entertainment itself. I drank my fill of her clenched fists, her popping eyes, her expression of fierce concentration, and then I took pity on her, loaded the sponge with warmer soapy water and began to wash her skin.

I loaded her breasts and belly with wetness and warmth, bubbles and scent, brushing the sponge into every crease and dimple until I reached her pubic triangle.

"Let's get you nice and clean," I said under my breath. "And ready. Ready for your treatment."

I made sure the sponge was extra soapy before dabbing it between her thighs, covering every pore in a slow upward sweep until I reached her poor neglected pussy lips. Three days was the longest time they had gone without the introduction of fingers, tongue or cock since we'd found each other and the resulting shadow of stubble was dark around that deep red split. I let the foam-charged sponge part the lips and enjoyed her small spasm once the stinging soap met delicate flesh.

"Oh, dear. You moved. Legs wider, please; I think we'll need a little more attention to this area."

She was brave, so brave and so obedient, and she didn't resist or protest but opened up to let her tormentor farther in, bearing my increased chafing of her clit with a squirming, gasping version of fortitude.

I picked up a razor. "I hope I don't need to tell you that you are forbidden to strain your voice." I traced straight lines of bare skin across her mons. "Any crying out or making a sound will be met with punishment."

I hoped she would bear this in mind. I really didn't want any damage to her voice, and I would have to take care not to go too far with this scene, welcome as it was.

Putting the razor aside, I ordered her onto her stomach.

Washing her from shoulder blades to the curve of her back, I gathered myself for the main event, drawing closer and closer to the part of her body I had missed the most. Up the hill, down the valley, I let water gush into the crack, wetting her bottom until it gleamed and shone like a pair of pale pearls.

I discarded the sponge and slipped a finger and thumb down between her cheeks, drawing them apart to spread them and expose her anus.

"Now about that fever. We need to make sure your temperature's down before we go any farther." I dipped the forefinger of my free hand into an open jar of lubricant and then inserted it slowly and patiently into Loveday's tensing little rosebud, opening it up, preparing it. Once she had stopped gasping, I reached for my instrument.

"Most patients would have their temperatures taken with a digital ear thermometer," I told her, watching the slender glass wand slide inside her asshole, deeper and deeper. "But not you. You're different, Loveday. You need special treatment. It says so in your notes."

"Does it?" she whispered.

"Yes, it does." The thermometer was all the way in now. I rotated it slowly, making her feel it, still holding her cheeks spread with that thumb and finger. "It says *Patient needs firm handling at all times. Facilitate her swift recovery with frequent rectal examinations and strict discipline.* The consultant seems very sure that this is what you need."

"Stupid consultant."

I was sure she intended me to hear the words and I raised my eyebrows, not that she could see, and pulled the thermometer out quickly and cleanly, watching her sphincter contract in confusion.

"What was that?" I inspected the reading. Normal! Hallelujah. "I see from my thermometer that you are not too ill for a spanking, young lady. Disrespecting the consultant certainly merits one. In fact, I think he should be here to witness it...but I think he's on another call. Never mind. You can imagine him here, and I'll write up a report on your punishment, just so he knows."

Her ankles and wrists twisted and I watched her make all her familiar preparations for what was to come, tensing her buttocks and shoulders, lifting her neck, all the better to grit her teeth. But I had an extra challenge for her today.

I retrieved the sponge, lifted it high over her bottom and let the water pour, splish splash splosh, all over the target area.

Once she was soaked and covered with droplets, I let my hand fall, hard, onto the crest of her bum. The sound it made was different, a splat rather than a smack, and her reaction was interesting, too. She almost reared up. It had been a long time since she'd done that, a long time since I had been able to surprise her with pain. Visions of pleasant future experiments floated before my eyes—wet paddlings, strappings, canings, all the flagellant variations my fertile imagination could devise.

I chuckled. "That's how it feels on a wet bottom. I'd heard it's more painful. Now I know it's true."

I had to find out how long it would take to dry her out using the warmth and air generated by my palm. Drops bounced off and back again, and the process took a surprisingly but delightfully long time, so I shouldn't have been disappointed when she began to show signs of discomfort, rolling around and kicking up her legs.

By the time the last patches of damp had evaporated, she was the ripe red of Snow White's poisoned apple and generating enough heat to power her bedside lamp for an hour or two.

I gave the hot seat a rub. "There," I said. "A red, sore bottom is very good at aiding recovery for minxes like you. I think we'll repeat that prescription thrice daily."

"Thrice," she croaked. "But it hurts."

"The best medicines are hard to swallow." The word "swallow" went straight to my groin, swelling my already-hard cock. "Speaking of which...but no. I can't be sure the infection has cleared up yet. We'll have to find another way of administering the dose."

"The dose?"

"The medicine you need," I whispered into her ear. "The medicine you're going to get."

"Can I ask for a second opinion? Ouch."

My second opinion lit up her roasted bum all over again, then I reached under the bed for the cuffs.

"It's an unorthodox treatment," I told her. "I'm writing up my findings for the medical journals. It's proving very effective, but it can be a little difficult to administer if the patients are too mobile. So..."

I cuffed a wrist, securing it to the nearest bedpost.

"...I think restraints are in order, but it's nothing to worry about."

She looked so good bound and at my mercy, her small hands balled into tentative fists.

"It's all perfectly safe," I continued. "Trust me. I'm a doctor. Now, get up on your knees and spread them."

She slid and slipped about on the sheet, trying to uncurve her spine while the chains held her taut, carefully widening her thighs until that sweet cunt split open, exposing its rich red contents to my view.

"If you make a sound, the treatment will be ineffective and I will have to use something stronger on that sore bottom of yours. So complete silence for this, understand?"

Her voice needed protecting. There was to be none of her moaning and whimpering today. I picked up a vibrator, an old favorite, shaped and sized just right for her. Would she be able to take this in silence? It would be fun to find out.

"It's called orgasm therapy," I said, placing the tip of the vibrator at her tight little hole. "Come-valescence." I almost wanted to apologize for that.

"Oh, that's terrible," she said, which was true, but didn't mean that she would get away with her impertinence. I sent the vibrator on its merry way with a firm shove, causing her to gasp and writhe in her chains.

"I said silence. That's five strokes of the strap for you later."
The rest of the vibrator glided in to the hilt. I looked at its wide base, lurking snugly below the stretched flesh of her cunt, for a while, admiring it, before flicking the switch and turning it on.

It hummed quietly but, I think, effectively. Her breathing became labored quite quickly. I put on surgical gloves before moving a hand down underneath the invasive tool and finding her clit. Lovely and swollen it felt, ready to be made even wetter and fatter until my poor girl had no choice but to come, hard but silent, on my fingers. I know how she likes it and I gave her the deluxe version, the rubbing, the stroking, the teasing, the circling, the twist of the vibrator. She had no defense and her first orgasm was swift and luscious, her thighs trembling, reddened bottom jiggling; but would she break her vow of silence?

"You're coming, aren't you? That's good. Very good. Let it out. That's right." She panted heavily, but her vocal cords remained unused. She had passed the first test. "But we haven't finished yet."

I switched up the setting on the vibrator and attached a clit buzzer for good measure. My latexed fingers were sopping wet already, but I dipped them into the lubricant anyway, letting them draw a shiny trail up the crack of Loveday's ass until they reached their destination. Had she guessed where her medicine was to be administered? I left her in no doubt, probing slowly, painting her ring with lube until it gleamed, inviting me farther in.

"I think this is where the dosage will be given."

I parted the rounded cheeks, inspecting her closer, enjoying the residual warmth her well-spanked bottom transferred to my skin through the gloves. She offered me this tiny port of ingress willingly and frequently, but it never lost its powerful appeal.

Each time was new, taboo and rude as the first. I listed some words for it in my head...sodomy, buggery, ass-fucking: each perfectly, obscenely decadent. I was harder than ever, wanting to be lodged inside that dark tight place, but knowing that I had all the time in the world.

I put a finger through the barrier, enjoying as ever the little spasm of protest as it tightened around me, then I added another and scissored them, preparing her for something much meatier.

"Yes," I said, my voice sounding strange to me then, thick and coarse.

I couldn't wait. I unbuckled my belt, lowered my trousers, released the belligerent scoundrel from its bondage and took it in hand.

Shifting up behind her on the bed, my pelvis nudged the vibrator farther into her, feeling its waves of pleasant warmth through my groin, then I guided the tip of my cock toward its target, held open by those fingers, ready to be breached.

"Take your medicine," I whispered, and the tip bludgeoned its way in, slicking up with the lubricant as it went. I used to fret about tearing her, but I know her capacity now, and I know how hard and how fast I can take her, so I didn't spare her. I pushed forward without stopping when she flexed her hips in mild resistance, enjoying her tension and the straining I provoked. Tight, so exquisitely tight, I was clamped and held firm by that well-filled asshole of hers. I could live in there, I thought deliriously. Stay in there forever. Push her around like a wheelbarrow through the streets, ass and cock in permanent connection. God, why do I think these things?

She pushed back, that moment I always relish the most.

"That's good," I said, beginning to thrust, bumping the rounded head of the vibrator in her other passage with every forward motion.

Take your medicine, take your medicine.

She struggled against the devilish machinations of the vibrator and the clit buzzer, coming twice before I was ready to commit my final act of domination.

I seized her hips, feeling the imminent rush, that blanking-out of everything except the glory of fucking, of taking, of having, of possessing. Yes, she was mine; yes, she would always be mine; ass, cunt, body, soul: mine.

She fell forward onto the rubber sheet. I didn't know whether she had maintained that ordered silence, but I didn't much care either. She was damp with exertion, flushed and breathing hard, but she was well. She was better.

I kissed her spine from neck to coccyx, then, when my legs regained their normal solidity, I went to get a towel from the bathroom.

I patted her down, wiping her clean of sweat, lube and sex before uncuffing her and removing the rubber sheeting.

I brought her poor depleted body into my arms, holding it in a bundle. She trembled like a frightened animal.

"I think you need to go back to bed rest if we're going to continue this treatment."

I held her until the shaking subsided, then tucked her back into bed, taking her temperature for real this time.

"It's well down," I told her. "For some reason. I would have expected that kind of treatment to elevate it. But what do I know? I'm not a doctor."

"Hey," she croaked with mock-indignation. "You aren't? So...what was that?"

I grinned at her drowsy face.

"That was for your own good," I said. "Now I'm going to call your doctor and ask what he recommends for girls who are well enough to be taken vigorously up the ass, yet protest that they can't go back to work yet."

"No, you aren't, you swine!"

"Yes, I am. Or rather, no, I'm not. Because I know what he'd say. I know what he'd write on his prescription form. Something painful involving your behind and my hand, I suspect. So you'd better get some rest while I work my strength up."

She pouted a little then yawned.

"Thank you. You may not be a doctor, but I think I'm cured."

I kissed her forehead. She shut her eyes, halfway to sleep already.

"I'm very glad to hear it," I said. "Gladder than you know."

Yes, I hate it when she's ill. But nursing her back to health is one of my favorite projects.

APPLE BLOSSOMS

Emerald

T here they are," I said to Brooke, who pulled the straw from her mouth and waved at the group coming in the door. Our friend Scott waved back, and we alerted the staff and made our way from the bar to the rectangular table reserved for our group of eight. "Happy birthday, Bethany," I said to the guest of honor and Scott's wife, giving her a hug as we reached the table. Brooke echoed the sentiment, and there was a general shuffling of chairs as seven people discerned where to sit and placed their belongings accordingly.

"Courtney called and said she's on her way," Scott said to the table at large as Bethany seated herself at one end of it. "And Brooke and Ashley, I'd like you to meet Brad, one of Bethany's and my friends from our coed softball league. Brad, this is Brooke and Ashley." There was a hint of severity in the look Scott shot his friend as Brooke and I stepped forward to shake his hand.

Brad appraised us with barely disguised enthusiasm. "Nice

to meet you," he said, giving us both a once-over as he sat down across from the chair Brooke dropped into. As soon as I was seated, he said, "So, how long have you two been together?"

"About five years."

"Five years. Huh." Brad sat back in his chair. Scott had obviously told him about us, though I didn't know how much he'd said. I found out when Brad continued.

"So do you go both ways then, or just girls?" He addressed the question to both of us, and immediately I knew how to account for the look Scott had given him during the introductions.

"Is that a common icebreaker question of yours?" Brooke asked, her smile sedate.

"I just find you both hot," Brad responded as though that somehow constituted an answer. "I'd do both of you in a heartbeat, so I was just wondering what the chances were of my getting to join you in a threesome tonight." He winked, and I had little doubt the charm that emanated from his blue eyes had historically served him well in tempering a characteristic audacity.

"How interesting that you seem to assume that our relationship is nonmonogamous, and also that there's nothing inappropriate about intimating to both of us, in each other's presence, that you want to fuck her respective partner. Do you usually tell people you want to fuck them when their partner is sitting right there?" Brooke's tone was mild, and I knew she wasn't speaking antagonistically but rather capitalizing on an opportunity to enlighten.

Brad looked confused, then considered for a moment. He shrugged. "I guess you're right. Sorry."

I smiled, nudging Brooke's foot affectionately under the table. Brad's comment wasn't anything we hadn't heard the likes of before, but that didn't inoculate me from finding it annoying. One of the many things Brooke and I had in common was a keen interest in the demolition of sexual and gender stereotypes, superficial assumptions about lesbian relationships being high on the list.

It happened that Brooke and I did not define our partnership as strictly monogamous, though our respective play beyond the relationship had tapered considerably in the last few years. While both our multi-partnered and kinky proclivities had flared with gusto during the first couple years we were together, for the past few such outside interaction had maintained a contented trickle. Our kinky play was now practiced almost solely between the two of us, and as often as not, our sex was vanilla.

But that was all by conscious and considered choice, and the inclination, desire and experience were still there for both of us if the opportunity arose. When Brooke caught my eye, there was a gleam in hers that I recognized. I held back a smile. The proposal I saw in them was something we hadn't done in a while, probably a couple years if I remembered correctly. But that gleam told me she felt the opportunity had arisen.

With my look back, I answered.

Brooke smiled and turned back to Brad. "As it happens, the two of us have occasionally engaged in such a configuration. But you may not feel comfortable with the kind of things Ashley and I have been known to incorporate into our sex life."

"Like what?" He was immediately interested again.

"Some things some people might consider a little rough. Bondage. Strap-ons."

"Well, I guess I'm not surprised you use strap-ons," he said with a lopsided grin, and I resisted the urge to roll my eyes. *Brad, Brad, Brad*, I thought. *You could really use a little bit of a wake-up call—as well as perhaps a crash course in sensitivity.*

Brooke was wearing a barely hidden smirk that anyone who knew her would recognize. Brad, of course, didn't know her, so his obliviousness continued as she spoke again. I sat with my glass in my hand, content, as was not uncommon, to let her do most of the talking. Despite the kinky and multi-partnered activities in my past, both with Brooke and before I met her, in both social and sexual settings I tended to be somewhat shy. Brooke and I switched, and I was fully capable of dominating her on occasion, but around groups and whenever more than the two of us had been involved, I was usually content to let Brooke lead the way.

"So we'd want anyone who joined us to be interested in those things, too," Brooke continued.

"Great!" Brad practically drooled into his beer, and I almost laughed out loud.

"You're comfortable with that kind of thing?"

"Yeah, whatever you want!"

Brooke's smile held just enough of an edge to let anyone listening know she was serious. "Don't you think you might want to be careful giving someone you don't even know that kind of carte blanche in a sexual setting?"

For the first time, Brad blushed, and I wondered what was really going on inside his head. I suspected what Brooke had in mind, and I suspected as well that Brad might not be as thrilled as he anticipated were he to be aware of it.

With that blush, for some reason, I wondered if I was wrong.

Scott turned our way then from the conversation he'd been having with the other half of the table. "And what's going on down here?" he asked with a swig of his drink, his gaze flitting from Brad to me to Brooke. Instantly he registered Brooke's expression, and his eyes went back to Brad. I saw the wariness in them as he let the question dangle, this visual assessment seeming to have increased his interest in the answer.

"Just getting to know each other," I said with a wink.

"I see. Can I get anyone another drink?" Scott stood up and glanced down at us as Brad and Brooke both relayed a request. I thanked him with a shake of my head, and he turned and headed for the bar.

Brooke engaged in answering a question from our friend Peggi, who was sitting on the other side of her, and Brad turned to respond to a comment from Bethany. Our interrupted conversation slid away like a silk scarf slipping from a table, and I sat back and sipped my drink. Scott returned and handed one glass to Brad and set another on the table before sliding a chair down to sit by me.

"How's it going?" he asked.

"Fine." I grinned at him.

"Is Brad acting like an ass?" The question made me laugh out loud, and Scott continued. "I mentioned you guys to him ahead of time specifically to ask him to not act like an idiot, as I've certainly seen him do. Seriously, has he said anything truly offensive? He's a good guy—just needs a little education about some things. But I'll certainly get him out of here if it's a problem."

I waved my hand dismissively. "No, it's no big deal. Brooke handled it."

Scott chuckled. "I don't doubt it," he said as he stood up. "All right, I just wanted to say hi." I waved as he squeezed between the chairs back to his seat at the other end of the table.

When the bill had been paid and the party started to break up, Brooke kissed my cheek as we stood to say our good-byes. Catching Brad staring, she looked directly at him and said, "Would you like to come with us, Brad?"

"Hell, yeah." Brad almost dropped his glass in his rush to

set it down. He stood up, a cocksure demeanor indicating that perhaps he really had assumed the invitation would be forthcoming all along. I shook my head to myself.

"You're ready to join in however we ask? Because I can assure you, Brad, you won't just be watching." Brooke's smile was calm, her gaze on Brad steady.

"Of course I want to join in." He looked as if she'd asked if he'd be willing to win the lottery, and I spoke up.

"Even if what we do seems a little...unorthodox?"

He grinned at me, his blue eyes sparkling as he said, "You bet, sweetheart. I'd love the chance to get into whatever you two have going on."

I saw Brooke's smile widen. She gave him a nod, and I turned and followed as she led the way to the door.

Brad may not have bargained for the position he found himself in two hours later in our spare bedroom, but I knew Brooke felt the same way I did: the second he wasn't enjoying it, it wouldn't be happening.

Once away from the scene at the restaurant, Brad appeared a little nervous, as well as unsure. Despite his enthusiasm, I didn't doubt that he had no idea what to do after he followed us into the entryway of our home. Of course, even if he had, what I knew Brooke had in mind would likely have looked considerably different from what he expected.

After going over safewords and the talk about everything being consensual, Brad began to resume the boldness we had observed at the table.

"Great," he said as he sat back against the living room couch with a grin. "So you two are just going to go at it then, and I'll join in as soon as I can't stand it anymore and finish the job?" He gave me a wink, and I smiled back at him.

Before Brooke could speak, I did it for her: "I don't think that was quite the way we were seeing it."

He raised his eyebrows, the smile still in place, and said, "Well, let me in on the secret, then, ladies. How do you picture this going down?"

Brooke smiled as she stood up. "I'm glad you asked, Brad. Follow me, please."

She led the way into the spare bedroom, flicking on the low lamp on the bedside table. In the middle of the room was a spanking bench covered in burgundy leather padding. She pulled a coil of silver rope from the chest at the foot of the bed.

In the low light, Brad did indeed looked a bit taken aback. "Wow. So which one of you gets tied up?" he asked, looking at the two of us.

Brooke chuckled softly. "Neither."

Confusion flickered over Brad's face for an instant before understanding replaced it, and for the first time, he looked unabashedly surprised. There was silence in the room for several seconds.

"What happens then?" Brad's voice was thick.

"We'll show you," Brooke said, lifting a pair of harnesses from the chest before handing me my realistic-style dildo from it. Brad watched as she retrieved her own jet-black silicone toy and closed the chest. "I'll give you a hint, though: These strap-ons may not be put to quite the use you were envisioning during our earlier conversation."

Brad's eyes widened, and I knew this was the moment of truth: the make or break time when he agreed or not, when he had the absolute option to stop this train before it started and walk right back out the door. The heat in the room seemed to elevate as we watched him. I truly had no idea what he would choose.

When he moved forward, his eyes on the bench, I suddenly remembered his blush at the restaurant. The memory checked the surprise I felt as he ran his fingers over the burgundy padding and slowly began to take off his shoes.

Brooke rested a hand now on the small of Brad's back as she positioned the black dildo between his buttocks. She rubbed it back and forth against his opening, the liberally applied lube further smearing along his skin.

It was I who was watching, though not for long. I stood in front of Brad, who was draped over and bound to the bench in the center of the room. I was almost naked, wearing only my black demi bra and a harness to which the silicone dildo Brooke had handed me was secured.

Brooke ran her fingers over Brad's hips, waiting, among other things, for his muscles to relax. I watched as she spoke to him in soft tones, holding the dildo firm against his opening. Her chest was flushed, her skin dewy beneath the vinyl harness I hadn't seen her wear for a while.

She looked up and met my eyes. I caught my breath as desire sizzled through me.

Knowing she was waiting for me, I moved forward, as though to get closer to her, though it was Brad's mouth I was approaching. I maintained eye contact with my girlfriend until I felt the heat from Brad's breath against my thighs. Still looking at her, I set my hand on his head. His blond hair was smooth beneath my fingers.

With a little grin, Brooke broke eye contact and looked down at the back of Brad's head. I dropped my eyes to where he looked up at me. His gaze was wary, but beneath the humility I saw a hunger. It was that hunger—the part beneath the façade, beneath what he displayed regularly and perhaps even consciously knew was there—that I looked back at as I called it forth silently, waiting as it overtook the last bit of hesitation in his eyes. Whether this was something he would have thought he'd wanted, whether he would want it in an hour, or next week, or ever again under any circumstances besides those that had coalesced into this moment, I didn't know. I'd guess he didn't, either.

But the look in his eyes as he looked up at me said he wanted it now. And that was all I needed.

I looked up at Brooke and nodded. She set a hand on Brad's body and eased the black dildo into him. A sound came from his throat, and she pushed in farther at the same measured pace before withdrawing just as slowly. I watched as she continued to penetrate him slowly, waiting for him to get used to the sensation, for them both to grow comfortable with the rhythm. Heat simmered inside me as I watched the smooth motion of Brooke's strong hips.

I tightened my grip on Brad's soft hair as I looked back down at him. With my other hand, I grasped the silicone cock strapped to my body and touched it to his lips. They opened easily, and I groaned as though there really were nerve endings in the toy connected to me as I slid it into his mouth. My pussy tingled, arousal gathering in my clit as I pulled my hips back and slid them forward again slowly. Like Brooke, I was finding the rhythm, and while fucking his mouth certainly didn't require the same delicacy as fucking his ass, I was pretty sure he wasn't used to this and didn't want to overwhelm him.

Brooke sped up her pace, observing Brad's muscles closely. I knew she was watching for any tension, anything that would indicate that he wasn't enjoying himself or that would cause discomfort as he took what she was giving him.

"Are you enjoying yourself, Brad?" she asked as she smacked his ass. "Are we making all your fantasies come true?" Her face had broken a sweat, her stylishly cropped blonde hair damp around her ears. The vision of her confident handling of Brad as well as her own obvious arousal had my pussy nearly dripping.

"I think he's liking it more than he may admit," she said to me, leaning down to reach beneath his body just behind the bench. She sent me a wink that pooled the heat between my legs further, and I jammed the dildo into Brad's mouth, careful not to hurt him, as I found a rhythm that made the base of the silicone press against my clit just so.

I moaned as I moved my body closer and closer to orgasm. In seconds, I screeched and bucked wildly as I came, backing away from Brad and sliding my fingers beneath the harness to replace the rhythm my bucking hips had created. Circling my clit frantically, I dropped to my knees as the climax tore through me, toppling my ability to stand.

I opened my eyes and looked across at Brooke, who had slowed down her own action to take in the view of my orgasm. The heat from her gaze seared into me, and I fell forward, panting, as my hand dropped slowly from my body.

I moved my eyes to Brad, whose gaze shot pure lust back at me as he took in my postorgasmic state like a lion feasting on flesh. Brooke looked down at him as well, clasping his hips as she steadied herself and prepared to pull out.

"Have you had about enough, darling?" she asked him. She backed up, removing the toy from his ass, and unfastened her harness. Her face was glowing with exertion and arousal, her blonde hair clamped to her forehead in little wet clusters. She was out of breath, her slim figure heaving as she removed the harness and stood still, allowing her body to regain its equilibrium.

She looked gorgeous.

I watched her from my knees as she stepped forward and

began to undo the rope around one of Brad's ankles. Momentarily I rose to help, allowing my breasts to dangle inches from his face as I undid one of the knots binding his wrists. I looked down to find his eyes glued to my tits, his breath audible as I untied the other wrist and Brooke invited him to stand up.

He stood in front of us, an unquestionable humility reflected in his eyes, his chest moving perceptibly as he finished catching his breath. I dropped my eyes to his granite-hard cock. A drop of precome glistened on the end of it, and I couldn't help smiling. Cocks didn't do a lot for me in and of themselves, but it was fun to be involved with someone's so obvious and acute arousal. I looked at Brooke, no idea what was on the agenda now.

"It looks to me like you want to get off. I guess that makes sense—that's what this little escapade was all about for you, wasn't it?" Brooke smiled cheerfully at Brad, who blushed a little as he swallowed. "Do you want to come?" Brooke asked when he remained silent.

Brad nodded, hurriedly, as though the answer was obvious but he had been afraid to state it. Which, I guessed, was exactly the case.

Brooke indicated his cock, a slow grin encompassing her features. "Go ahead."

He looked at her hesitantly. I looked at her, too. Brooke stood back, arms crossed, and I finally understood that she was prompting him to jack himself off while we watched.

I bit my lip, suddenly eager for something I had never found the slightest bit appealing. I wondered if it would please Brooke, and I realized that possibility was part of what turned me on.

Brad seemed to be waiting for further direction—either that, or he felt reluctant to start with our watching him. Ignoring him, I sidled over to Brooke and pressed against her naked body. I whispered into her ear, and she gave me a surprised smile. I blushed, knowing I seemed out of character—not just in the action I suggested but also in initiating, in wanting to do something different and impulsive like I watched her enthuse over all the time.

"Well, that's great, Ashley," Brooke said out loud. "Why don't you go right ahead and do that." She turned to Brad. "Ashley wants to kneel in front of you and have you come all over her tits." She ran a hand over my breast, squeezing lightly, and I ducked my head shyly.

I leaned forward and kissed her, briefly, and as I started to pull away she grabbed me and pulled me back toward her with a kiss that started fast and hard, her lips and tongue and mouth surging against mine, and transformed gradually and organically into the softness I saw in her sometimes, when her blonde hair became like a gentle light illuminating a face not devoid of her usual boisterousness but incorporating into it a sincerity, a gentle and exquisite caring. It wasn't something foreign to her—even when it didn't appear to be there, I knew it was, as an integral part of her that simply tended to stay quieter than the impulsiveness and enthusiasm—but whenever I experienced it so openly, so close to the surface like this, it was like being wrapped in emotional velvet, a softness exuding from her to me to everything around us, holding all of it in a lightness that, for a moment, overtakes the world.

When she had first grabbed me, I'd wondered if the kiss was partly for Brad's benefit, and whether it had been or not, by the end I knew it was for no one's—not even ours. It wasn't a "benefit" kind of kiss. It was just something that happened, like the opening of an apple blossom.

I opened my eyes slowly after we broke apart. With a soft smile, Brooke released my hands, which she'd been holding, and turned slowly back toward Brad. I followed suit, and he met my eyes as I looked at him, standing motionless with his hand positioned around his cock. His eyes shot fiery lust, and it occurred to me that he had just gotten a little bit of what he had originally wanted. I wondered if it had the same effect following his recent experience.

Holding his gaze, I stepped forward until I was almost touching him. He looked down at me, his jaw clenching and unclenching as I felt the heat from his body sweep over and blend with my own. I reached back and unhooked my bra, sliding my hands around my sides as I nudged the garment from my breasts and let it drop to the floor. His eyes fell to my tits, and he swallowed as he looked back up at me. For a moment, neither of us moved.

I dropped to my knees. Brad groaned, his head falling back as he gripped his cock tight in a fist, barely jerking it twice before his hot come shot straight onto my exposed tits, his volume increasing as he looked back down to see my fingertips sliding delicately over the slickness on my skin, watching the glistening surface with fascination as his face contorted and his hand tugged desperately at his cock. Automatically, he reached to put a hand on my shoulder for balance but caught himself before he did. Understanding his hesitation, I smiled and reached for his hand, bracing my palm against his to help hold him up as his last drops of come landed on my body.

Unexpectedly, I felt Brooke grasp my tits from behind, and I gasped. I turned my head to see her kneeling behind me, her lips hot against the back of my neck as her hands smeared through the come covering my chest to squeeze my nipples. A tiny whimper escaped me, and I let go of Brad's hand as my girlfriend grasped my body and devoured my neck with an urgency I felt suddenly on fire to experience once the two of us were alone.

Gradually Brooke released me, landing one more kiss at the top of my spine before she stood and reached to help me up. Brad stood, panting, in front of us, his expression a stupor of release and incredulity.

"Well, Brad, it's been a pleasure," Brooke purred, standing close to him as she looked up into his eyes. "I hope you enjoyed yourself."

Brad looked like he didn't know how to respond, or perhaps had not yet recovered his faculty of speech, and I stepped forward to rest a hand on Brooke's hip.

"Thanks for joining us," I said. "It had been a while since we'd done that."

"Really?" Brad let slip a moment of vulnerability, and he blushed. "I mean, have you...you've done that before?"

"Not quite like that." Brooke smiled. "You were a first."

Brad smiled, too, and I sensed the moment when all façades among us dropped. "It was a first for me, too," he said quietly. He turned to gather his clothes, and Brooke and I stood still as we watched him begin to dress.

Then she turned to me silently, pressing her body to mine with a kiss that instantly reignited the heat that rushed to my pussy. I slid my hands up her body and cupped her breasts, sensing her breath catch as I squeezed them, gently at first, then more firmly.

We were breathless as we broke apart. I turned to Brad, who was facing us as he fastened his belt.

"Thank you both," he said. His nod seemed a bit wistful, and I knew he was aware that Brooke and I were going to continue without him after he was gone—and that he understood why he wasn't invited. I knew also that it was an understanding that wouldn't have occurred to him a few hours before, and it endeared him to me.

I stepped forward to give him a hug. "It was very nice to meet you, Brad."

He smiled down at me, and I felt understanding in Brooke's hand as she took mine as we followed him to the door.

"Perhaps you could come back and play with us again sometime," she said as we reached it, giving my hand a squeeze.

I squeezed back as Brad turned around. "I'd love to," he said, his smile the most sincere I'd seen from him. Brooke and I stepped forward to give him a kiss on either cheek, and he waved and slipped out the door.

"Funny how much more likable he was after he was humbled," Brooke said.

"Most of us are," I answered, already pulling my girlfriend back toward the bedroom. "Come, my love. We've got a job to finish."

BIG NIGHT

D. L. King

I wanted Dan's fortieth birthday to be special, a day special enough to not tell our grandchildren about.

Dan and I met sophomore year in college, in a truly boring lecture class. I was sitting one row up, directly behind him. At some point, in the middle of the lecture, he dropped his pen and bent down to retrieve it. It was then that I noticed a flash of red peeking out from the top of his jeans. Not just red; it was lacy red. That was it for the lecture. To this day, I have no idea what it was about. It was a sociology class, that much I know, but the topic of the lecture completely escapes me.

Dan thinks it's pretty funny. He claims to remember it vividly—something about some experiment in Appalachia. But then, he was Anthro-Soc, and into all that stuff, and he wasn't the one looking at the lacy, red panties on the boy in front of him. I was Poli-Sci, taking the class because it fit into my schedule, and I couldn't think about anything other than the boy in front of me at that point.

I followed him out of the lecture hall at the end of class,

took his arm and asked if he wanted to have lunch. Back then, I knew what turned me on but was still learning how to go about getting it. I just went for it with Dan, knowing I couldn't let him get away. And we've been together ever since.

What does Dan like?

Dan likes exhibitionism. He likes humiliation, at least when it comes from me. He likes the danger of exposure, of being found out.

What do I like?

I like giving Dan what he likes. And I've been giving it to him ever since I stuck my hand down the back of his pants on the way to the cafeteria and ran my finger under the lace of his thong's waistband. Ooh, just thinking of that first experience with him gets me wet.

From that first day, after class, we were inseparable. We got an apartment together after graduation and played a lot of sexy games. We found some like-minded people and kept expanding our sexual horizons. We got married. We finished grad school, got jobs, bought a better apartment, had a couple of brilliant, beautiful kids, bought a house—just like everybody else—and continued to expand our horizons.

So, party? Absolutely. Two parties? Definitely. The first party would be for family and work friends. Dinner and presents, finishing up early, in time for the *other* party.

The second party would be with our favorite "expanded horizon" friends. There'd be presents and cake and champagne—and games.

It would be a surprise, all of it. I'd never given Dan a surprise party, and I figured it would be fun. It was all coming together in my mind. He'd be surprised by the family party and then wouldn't be expecting anything else, so the second party would be an even bigger surprise.

I spoke with his mother and she helped me plan the family party. I asked that it start at five-thirty, saying we had concert tickets for later. She was fine with that. We organized a great dinner and invited a mix of family and friends, a couple of whom would also be joining us for the second party.

We booked one of our favorite family-style Italian restaurants, the kind of place that had long tables, brought the food on large platters to pass around and served the wine in juice glasses. Home-style, savory goodness.

The second party would take place at our house. I called Carol, one of my closest friends, and asked her to be in charge of the setup for the house party, since we'd be out, and have to stay out, until it was time for Dan to be surprised again. She agreed to help and we sent out invitations to our kinky friends.

Finally, the big night came. The kids had left for sleepaway camp two days earlier. Carol had keys to the house. I'd made all my preparations and told Dan I'd spring for dinner and we were out the door.

On the way to dinner, I mentioned that as a birthday present, I'd bought tickets to see one of his favorite bands, and we'd be heading there after dinner. That got him excited. Heading downtown, I asked Dan where he'd like to eat. His response was the usual: *I don't know. Where do you want to go?* We batted around a few ideas and then I said, "Hey, look! There's Braccos. We haven't been there in a long time. How about that?"

Pulling up to the curb, I told him to park the car and I'd see if I could get us a table. I jumped out of the car before he had time to complain. I watched him slide over and went inside to let the hostess know we were there. Everything was ready.

When Dan came in, we followed the hostess to the back room where he practically jumped out of his skin when everyone yelled surprise. After he'd made the rounds and had his first cocktail, I wrangled him into a corner by the bathrooms. "Were you surprised?"

"Oh, yeah. I can't believe you did all this," he said.

"Well, your mother helped." I reached into my purse and handed him something. "Be a good boy and take care of this for me, will you?" His mouth opened wide but before he could say anything, I continued, "Oh, wait. And here; put these on, too." I pulled out a black lace thong and handed it to him. He immediately crumpled it up and stuffed everything into his pocket. I could see my little additions were having the desired effect on him, especially right after mentioning his mother. This was going to be fun.

After a long pause, he said, "But what about the concert?"

"Nobody's going to see your underwear at the concert."

"Yeah, I know, but—what about the—other thing?"

"Well, I'll make a decision about that when the time comes. Hurry up, honey. You need to get back to your guests." I gave him a peck on the lips and pushed him off toward the bathroom. Once he was gone, I rejoined the party.

Almost a full fifteen minutes later, Dan reappeared. I chased him down and put my arm around his shoulder and led him to the tables. "You feeling all right, honey?" I asked. "I was beginning to worry. It's time to order." I slid my hand down his back and over the swell of his ass, moving a finger between his cheeks to feel for, and push on, the butt plug now seated in his rear. "And don't think I don't know what you were doing in there all this time," I whispered before smacking his butt.

Before taking seats together in the middle of the main table, his mother asked him if he was feeling all right. I could see the blush begin in the middle of his cheeks, but he assured her he was fine.

Dan gingerly sat down and I pulled his thigh next to mine.

"Open your legs, baby. Get comfortable," I said, so everyone could hear. "You're the birthday boy. Take as much room as you need." I looked at the guests. "He's just so polite," I said.

Under the table, I curled my fingers around his thigh just at his crotch, leaned in to him and whispered, "Spread 'em." His blush deepened. His mother said something about wondering if he'd had too much to drink. "Not to worry," I said. "I'm the designated driver."

The food was great and plentiful and the waiters kept everyone's wineglasses filled. Taking my role seriously, I only had one glass of wine, knowing I'd be able to do more celebrating later. Whenever Dan looked like he was getting too comfortable, I'd ask him to reach over to pass me the salt, or lean back and relax, knowing the movements would wake the sensations in his ass. And whenever his mother would ask him a question, I'd stroke his cock through his jeans, or knead his balls. Being Dan, all this attention kept a continuous smile on his face, even if he occasionally became inarticulate.

After a cheesecake with a candle in it and singing "Happy Birthday," someone reminded Dan about the sizable pile of presents awaiting him. Unfortunately, since we had tickets, I said, we'd have to take them home with us for later, but we thanked everyone profusely.

As people started to leave, poor Dan, with his half-erect cock, had to get up and say good-bye to everyone, smiling and blushing the whole time. Because his jeans were fairly tight, I don't think people really noticed. Of course, I did—and Dan knew I did, as he cast glances my way from time to time. I smiled and nodded to him as I said good-bye to our friends as well.

Sharon and Bill, the couple who would be joining us later, came up to say good-bye. Sharon gave Dan a hug and whispered, "I've been watching you blush all night. Just what has

Laura been putting you through?" She stroked the edges of his ears, knowing it was an erogenous zone for him. "I can't begin to imagine. Well, that's not true. I'm sure I could imagine." I saw his cock jump in his pants.

When we left, Dan must have been too stimulated to remember to ask about taking the plug out of his ass, which I wouldn't have allowed, anyway. We got to the car and I made a big production of looking through my purse.

"Sweetie, I can't believe it, I must have left the tickets at home. We'll have to go back to get them."

"But we'll miss the opening band."

"It's okay," I said. "They're probably crap, anyway."

"Well, at least now I'll be able to take this plug out of my ass," he said.

"Maybe." He shot me a look. "Just think how interesting the bass will feel, vibrating through the plug," I said and kissed him. "By the way, are those wet spots on your jeans? Think anyone noticed?" I started the engine and began to drive.

All the way up the walk from the driveway, he kept trying to make deals with me to let him take the plug out. I gave him a wilting look and turned the key in the lock, pushing him through the open door. The lights came on and everyone yelled surprise and this time, I thought he might actually pass out.

He looked over his shoulder at me. "Does this mean there's no concert?"

I prodded him farther into the entryway and closed the front door behind us. The guys had moved most of the living room furniture out of the way and set up various pieces of dungeon equipment. Food and drinks were set out in the dining room. There was a big banner hanging over the fireplace that said HAPPY 40TH DAN with multicolored balloons on either side and a table piled high with presents.

Someone put a drink in Dan's hand and about that time, Sharon and Bill arrived.

"Was he surprised?" Sharon asked.

"Oh, my god," I said. "He was stunned. I think he's still in shock."

Someone started to chant the word "presents" and soon everyone picked it up. "I think they want you to open your presents, honey," I said.

"They're still out in the trunk."

"No, not those presents, these presents." I gestured to the table of gifts in the living room. Dan's eyes opened wide. I don't think he'd noticed them before.

George handed him a box wrapped in purple paper with pink bunnies. "Here, open this one first. It's from Sandy and me."

"First things first," I said. "Dan, you asked me for a favor? You'll have to take your clothes off first." Dan looked at me. "Well, didn't you say you wanted to take the plug out of your ass? You'll have to take your pants off to do that, won't you? Go ahead, I'm sure our friends won't mind waiting." Dan blushed wildly. "Take the shirt off, too, baby. You'd look silly with a shirt on and no pants." One of the guests snickered.

Dan unbuttoned his shirt and tossed it in the corner. He unbuttoned his jeans and pushed them down his thighs to whistles and catcalls as the black lace thong was exposed.

"Take off the shoes and socks so you can get the pants all the way off. You're keeping your guests waiting. Honestly, sometimes you can be so slow." My words began to have the desired effect on his cock, which began to rise, pushing the thong out. "Look at that sweet, little thing. Isn't it adorable?" Everyone laughed as my husband's cock pushed the thong completely away from his body.

"All right, bend over so I can remove the plug."

"But honey," Dan said, "not here."

"Why not here? You said you wanted it out. Come on. You're keeping our friends waiting. Don't be rude." Dan turned three shades of purple but slid the underwear over his fully erect cock and down his thighs and bent over, with his hands on the edge of the table. I reached down and stroked his ass before pulling out the plug to expose his nicely stretched asshole. "All right dear, you can pull your panties up now."

George held out his present again. "I think this is a good one to get things started," he said.

Dan opened it and started laughing. "Anal Ring Toss, why didn't I guess?"

I told Dan to kneel on the floor with his butt in the air. Deciding to leave the panties on, I pushed the scrap of fabric to the side and with the help of some lube, produced from a guest's pocket, I inserted the new plug into Dan. A black rod stuck up about a foot from his ass.

"Everyone gets a turn," I said, handing out the three bright yellow rings. The first to make it gets to play with the birthday boy." The game wasn't so easy. It took two rounds before anyone got their ring over the pole. The whole time I told Dan how cute he looked with his balls threatening to fall out of the thong. He was grinning from ear to ear when I finally removed the ring-toss plug and he stood up.

Since Sabrina won the game, she brought her present over to Dan next. It was a set of nipple clamps, which she applied to his chest. She led him over to the spanking bench set up in the living room and gave him a birthday spanking. I think it was hearing the spanking that got things started. Clothes were soon shed and people began to play.

When the spanking was finished, Sharon and Bill, probably

our closest friends, held out a package. The box contained a bunch of black straps and a purple dildo. "What is this?" Dan asked.

"Oh, honey, I think that's for me." I took the box upstairs and changed into my black leather bustier and panties and attached the strap on to my hips. The purple dildo jutted out from my pubic bone at a jaunty angle as I walked back downstairs. The party was in full swing and Dan was up against the St. Andrew's cross, getting flogged with a new flogger.

I waited until the flogging was finished and then ordered Dan to turn around and face me. His eyes got big.

"Oh. Ohhh."

"Time for everyone to watch me fuck you," I said. He was still wearing the lace thong but his cock was all the way out of it now and standing away from his body. "Look what you've done to those nice panties," I said. "It's too bad you don't know how to take better care of your things. Come over here."

Dan walked to me, his erection jiggling with each step. I slid my fingers under the waistband and snapped the lace apart, letting the thong fall to the floor before I ordered him back over the spanking bench.

I ran my hands over his hot little rear and said, "My darling husband is forty years old tonight—"

"But I'm not for—"

I smacked his ass. "Yes, yes, I know, you're not forty for another two days. I'll amend my earlier statement." I started again. "My darling husband is coming to the end of his thirties and will soon be completely and irrevocably over-the-hill." Dan started to get up, but I put my hand on his back. Everyone laughed. "As some of you may know, Dan's a bit of an exhibitionist." That got a few more guffaws from the audience and a, "Hey, now," from Dan.

"I'm talking now," I said and gave his bottom another smack, which got another round of laughter from the group. "As I was saying before I was so rudely interrupted"—I punctuated the last word with another smack—"my darling husband would like nothing better than to show off in front of his friends and so, to make his birthday the big night it should be, I've decided that you should all bear witness to his very first ass fuck. I know it's what he would want—if I were to give him a choice. Now, does anyone have some lube?" Four bottles were thrust toward me from the crowd. I chose one and nodded my thanks. "Oh, and thank you very much, Sharon and Bill, for my lovely new—er—Dan's lovely new strap-on. What a thoughtful gift!" More laughter. "By the way, birthday spankings will take place immediately after his ass has been well and truly reamed."

I drizzled lube onto Dan's exposed asshole. He squirmed from the sensation until I began rubbing it in with two fingers. I smoothed the lube inside him and added more before beginning to gently explore his opening. After sliding my index finger all the way in and slowly fucking him with it for a bit, I added more lube and inserted a second finger. That brought some complaining noises from Dan and a tensing of his muscles. I stilled. After all, I wanted this to be as pleasurable as he'd always dreamed it would be.

"Oh, now how do you expect me to fuck you with my cock if two slender little fingers are too much for you," I chided. Once he relaxed again, I added more lube and started again. "There, now, that's better, isn't it?" I watched the death grip he had on the spanking bench begin to loosen and his hand leave the bar he'd been gripping. "Don't you dare touch yourself..." I said. His hand came back into sight. "...Until I tell you to."

By this time, he was getting into it and actively pushing back against my hand as I continued to fuck him. Withdrawing

my fingers brought real noises of complaint. As I put lube on
the dildo and added more to his ass, I said, "You're a whiny,
demanding brat, aren't you? I suppose I'll have to give you something to whine about, then," and I pressed the head of the dildo
against his anus. He grew still. "That's right," I said. I grabbed
his hips and slowly inched it in until it was balls deep. Stopping
there, I let him get a good feel for being completely filled.

Slowly I withdrew, until I was almost out of him before
pushing back inside, a little faster. I continued, faster each time,
until I was actively pumping him. When he began pushing back
against me with each of my thrusts, I told him he could touch
himself and his hand shot to his cock. He was working hard by
this time; we both were. His grunts and moans were escalating
as sweat pooled at the small of his back.

Beyond the stage of talking now, I watched his arm as the
muscle danced. He was jacking his cock with real intent. When
his motions became more erratic and his thrusts against me grew
more powerful, I slowed my fucking, but matched his intensity,
shoving my purple cock in harder and harder, trying to bury
myself, through the silicone appendage, inside my husband.
With a strangled cry, he came.

I stopped thrusting, staying still inside him, and watched
his muscles contract with each spasm of his orgasm. I heard
someone say, "Oh, yeah," and when he was finished, I slowly
withdrew.

He lay there for a while, panting, waiting for his heart rate
to slow.

"I hope you realize you're going to have to clean that up," I
said and watched as his body shook with his chuckles. I stroked
his back, leaned over him and kissed his neck before he turned
his head to kiss me properly. The guy looked completely spent.
He started to get up and I gently pushed him back down.

"Where do you think you're going?" I asked. "Your guests are waiting to give you your birthday spankings. What the hell kind of host are you, anyway?"

And it was true; our friends had indeed lined up, eagerly awaiting their turns. I removed the strap-on and went around to Dan's head. Kneeling in front of him, I stroked his damp hair and kissed him as the first spank landed.

"I love you," he mouthed before saying, "Ouch," to a particularly well-placed smack.

"Happy birthday. I love you, too," I said.

THE GUEST STAR

Sinclair Sexsmith

It is always different to fuck somebody new. New skin, new lips, new way she kisses, new way she writhes, new way she comes. I don't make a lot of assumptions the first time. I don't expect us to get off; I don't expect to be able to tell when she comes, if she does. I don't expect dirty talk, I don't expect a lot of communication about what's what. Of course I do my best at all of those things—but with someone new, you just never know. Maybe it's the chivalrous service top in me, but I watch for cues and tend to take them from her, as best I can.

Which is how I ended up stroking my cock, still wearing my T-shirt, my back up against the wall in my room, watching Kristen get fisted. By someone else.

After watching her get seduced.

Kristen and I had both noticed Gabrielle when we met her at a queer event a month or so before, so when she was in town this time, we made sure to make plans to meet up for a drink. *Who knows what will happen,* I told myself. Kristen told me she thought Gabrielle was pretty, and slutty and smutty and loudmouthed enough to be that big river of energy that Kristen often seeks in those close to her. Gabrielle was running late. No ETA exactly. When we went off to meet her, I was a little bit skeptical about whether she'd even show. "I half expect to get stood up," I joked. It wasn't that I didn't want to see Gabrielle. When I thought about it later, I realized it was because I had no part in setting up this date. Kristen and Gabrielle arranged it, and though Kristen texted me to ask where we should meet up (the dyke bar in Brooklyn, of course), I had almost no part in the asking, the saying yes, the gauging of how interested or not Gabrielle might be.

All night, I had trouble reading Gabrielle. I was interested and curious about her—she's a smart, hot femme who it seems can make anybody laugh. Her style is cute and chic. She's short, a little shorter than Kristen even, who is five foot two, and not thin but not so heavy, just enough that I want to grip the flesh on her thighs. She talks a lot and says interesting things about all sorts of topics—being poly, education, art. I'd liked her immediately when we'd met.

But I couldn't tell what was going to happen. I couldn't quite get a grasp on the conversation; I sometimes felt like the third wheel. I'd bring the conversation around to sex, but it didn't take long for Kristen and Gabrielle to start talking about other things, like the socioeconomic makeup of the cities in which they lived, or queer community friend politics.

I didn't try too hard. The conversation was interesting; I jumped in occasionally. Mostly, it was fun to watch them banter back and forth.

Kristen had just made a pie, so we had a good excuse to take Gabrielle back to our place for a slice of it. They talked more. It was getting late. Finally, they started making out on the couch.

Gabrielle pushed Kristen down and worked her hand between Kristen's legs. Kristen grasped at her back and shoulders and came once, twice.

"Can I take this off of you?" Kristen asked her, pulling at Gabrielle's dress.

"Somewhere darker," she answered, so we went into the bedroom.

They continued playing on the bed, stripping off their clothes. I wasn't exactly sure of my move...should I join? That would feel a little bit like forcing myself into the situation. Plus, I was really enjoying watching. I am usually so much closer to Kristen when she gets aroused, watching her skin flush while my hands are already on her body, and watching someone else do it was interesting, both puzzling and a thrill. They were adorable together, passionate in their kissing and grabbing handfuls of thigh and ass and tits.

I tried to be casual as I got out my favorite cock and slid off my jeans, still watching them kissing, touching, fucking on the bed. I stood against the wall, one hand on my cock, and watched as Kristen lay back on the pillows, one hand gripping the bars of the black headboard as she opened her thighs and pushed against Gabrielle's hand inside of her, as Gabrielle knelt between her knees.

I moved to sit on the edge of the bed up near the headboard, next to Kristen. Gabrielle's whole hand was inside of her, disappearing at the wrist. I reached for the lube and offered it to Gabrielle. She noticed my cock, ready, and laughed. Kristen noticed it too, and reached for it with her hands, stroking it while I lowered my mouth and kissed her. We managed a whispery check-in: "You okay?"

"So great." She told me she wanted my cock in her mouth. Gabrielle pulled out and Kristen shifted forward onto her knees, still on the bed. My bed is on risers, which makes the side of it at an almost perfect hip-height. I stood beside it as Kristen eagerly swallowed the length of me, sucking eagerly, mouth wet and wanting, making those little gulping sounds as she swallowed and sucked. Her back arched high as she was on her hands and knees, low enough to get to my cock at hip-level as I stood at the side, her knees apart, exposing her pussy to Gabrielle, who was behind her now, gripping her ass with both hands, smacking it a little, rubbing, until finally lowering her mouth down to Kristen's pussy.

Kristen moaned. She is one of those people who is not so good at the famous sixty-nine position, for example, because she gets too distracted by what's happening to her pussy to concentrate on what's in front of her mouth. I also know, however, that sometimes she doesn't have to concentrate on her mouth—I can just slide my cock in and out and use it like another hole to fuck. And so I did. Slid it in and out, gripped the back of her head gently while I pumped my hips, and Kristen went even more limp, relaxing, her body opening.

It didn't take long before she was shaking and crying out, muffled behind her full mouth, pressing her body back against Gabrielle and sputtering as she came. I lifted her mouth up to mine and she sat up high on her knees, kissing me.

"Get down," I told her. She shifted, knees still shaky, off of the bed so she stood next to it with me. I kissed her again and then quickly turned her around and bent her over the side of it, pressing her back with my hand and opening up her pussy with my other hand, guiding my cock in, so wet and easy, and started fucking her.

Gabrielle was on the other side of the bed, watching. A nice show for our guest.

I started slow with a few strokes to get my cock nice and

wet, then went for it, thrusting hard, not stopping, not too fast yet but hard, deeper, listening to her cry out, hands grasping for the bed, gripping the sheets and thrashing as I sped up, harder, moving the bed inches across the hardwood floor. I took a firm hold on her hips, then brought one hand around to her clit and she exploded, coming hard, squirting all over the side of the bed, down my legs, onto the floor.

Shaky, we disentangled and she climbed back up onto the bed where Gabrielle was waiting. I wiped down my legs quickly as they kissed again, curled up with each other.

What happened next is a little bit of a blur. Gabrielle relaxed a little, by which I mean she relaxed out of her toppy-ness and let us both touch her a bit more. I kissed Gabrielle, unhooked her bra and pulled off her panties as she lay on the bed next to Kristen. She seemed a little self-conscious, but I loved the sight of the curves of her, her small round belly, her thighs, her tits, a little larger than Kristen's but still close to the same size, both of them smaller than me but not exactly skinny. Enough flesh to grab on to, enough to grip, enough so that there was padding between us and I wasn't worried about being too heavy and accidentally doing some damage. I worry enough about damage as it is; I want to fuck a girl who, I can tell, can hold her own.

After I took Gabrielle's last pieces of clothing off, she lay back on the bed next to Kristen again and they kissed, touching each other, as I worked my fingers in Gabrielle's cunt, softly at first, just exploring, to see if she wanted to be touched, then harder and deeper as she opened up and spread her legs, breathing heavier and still kissing Kristen. She gasped a little as I worked in two fingers, then three. Kristen started writhing in response to Gabrielle: flushed, hips pushing against my hand. Kristen moaned, rubbing her thighs together and pressing closer to Gabrielle, stealing glances at me, which I took as an invitation and brought my left hand up to Kristen, too, finding her wet, happy to get touched again. Fingers in both of them, working in and out, slowly, easily, as Gabrielle gasped and they kept kissing, hands on each other everywhere, tongues in and out of each other's mouths.

"I think I want her to fuck me," Gabrielle finally said to Kristen.

"Oh?" Kristen asked back. "She *is* pretty good at that. I recommend it."

(This is the kind of banter we'd had all night.)

"That's how it seems!"

"You could ask for it."

"How?"

(*You guys, I'm sitting right here.* Also, *holy shit.*)

"You could say…'I want your cock.' Or you could say, 'Please fuck me.' Or you could say, 'Would you pretty please put that cock in my pussy?'"

Gabrielle finally turned to me. I was barely holding myself up on my knees and had leaned back against the footboard of the bed. "Would you please…fuck me?" she asked.

I tried to maintain my cool. "Uh, yes, of course."

"Would you use a different one? That one is too much."

"Sure." I was thinking I'd change cocks regardless; it's not so smart to share toys. I swapped out the harness and cock for a slightly smaller cock and rubber harness, which is easier to clean. I went over to the side of the bed Gabrielle was on and kissed her again, pulled her against me, ran my hands along her body to get used to touching her. Kristen watched. Gabrielle put one hand to my cock and looked at it, then looked up at me, and I pushed her back and pressed open her thighs, then slid inside her easily.

"Go slow," she urged. She doesn't get penetrated too often.

She's usually a top, I'd found out. That made more sense regarding why she was seducing Kristen, and why I was a little confused earlier. But she was the kind of top who liked to get fucked after topping, she said. Made for the best orgasms that way. I went slow. Gabrielle turned and embraced Kristen again, kissing more, their hands on each other's bodies, breasts, skin, as I knelt and grabbed Gabrielle's inner thighs, pulling us together and apart as I worked inside of her, lubed up my thumb and touched her clit.

"Fuck," she moaned, still kissing Kristen. I guessed I had the right spot. I didn't know her body, I couldn't quite tell. Soft, but a little faster, I kept going. "Fuck, *fuck*," she breathed, faster, swearing, "Oh, god, oh, god, oh," as I flicked my fingers against her clit and my hips against her, until she yelled a string of "*Fuck fuck fuck fuck!*" and let go of Kristen to grip the headboard, pushing against me, harder, laughing and flushed, skin pink with a thin layer of sweat.

"I come and you just keep going," she breathed. She didn't seem to mind, and wasn't pushing me away, but rather keeping me right there, rocking against me, her hips working in rhythm with mine. I laughed and let up.

Kristen was starry eyed, looking a little like someone had just thrown her a surprise birthday party, thrilled and thrown off. I detangled from Gabrielle and went over to the side of the bed where Kristen was and we three held each other, stroking our skin, laughing for a little while, until Gabrielle decided it was time to get going. We called a cab for her, walked her to the front door and called it a night.

EXPOSURE

Elizabeth Coldwell

The room is comfortably warm, with nibbles and dips arranged in bowls on the table. A jug of mojitos, heavy with rum and mint, waits to be served. Jason's tread is light as he descends the stairs barefoot. The stage is set.

In minutes, I will have placed him in the most deliberately humiliating position of his life. His desires laid bare, he will submit to me in the way he has so long desired. My pussy, already slick with anticipation, lets loose another trickle of cream into my panties at the thought. I can't wait for the game to begin.

The first time I saw Jason, I knew he'd look good naked. He was bending over a weight machine, adjusting the amount to be pressed, and in that position he gave me the most marvelous view of his taut ass, cycling shorts clinging to it like they couldn't bear to let go. If I hadn't already signed up for a six-month membership at the gym, that display alone would have persuaded me to do so.

Of course, I wasn't the only client who lusted after Jason.
All messy blond curls, bright white smile and easy charm, he
was the only personal trainer at the gym with a waiting list for
one-on-one sessions, and every single one of the names on that
list was not only female, but a good fifteen years younger than
I was. That's why I was so surprised when he started taking an
interest in how I was doing, encouraging me to put in one last
mile on the treadmill when my legs felt like they didn't have the
strength to drag me any farther, or helping me with my stance
as I worked on my arm muscles with the free weights. *Why me?*
I wondered, as his professional courtesy turned into something
more intimate. After all, he could take his pick of the clients,
so why not choose one of the hard-bodied beauties closer to his
own age?

I didn't know then about his worship of older women. Blame
it on the friend of his mother who seduced him as an innocent eighteen-year-old, leaving him hungry for the pleasures
provided by an experienced lover. Combine that with an inher-
ently submissive nature, and it's a blend few people can handle.

Not that I considered myself to be one of those people. When
Jason told me he was looking to be dominated, I immediately
thought of leather-clad mistresses, and all the clichés of whips
and chains that surround them. I didn't realize then how the
right words can be as cutting as any riding crop, how punishment doesn't need to include pain. All I know is that he saw
something in me I'd never seen in myself and slowly, gradually,
he brought it out.

The other reason he was so attracted to me was my feet.
They're so small I find it very hard to find suitable training shoes
in adult sizes, and as Jason watched me pounding on the treadmill, he recognized immediately I'd been shopping for footwear
in the children's department. My dainty size-threes pushed all

his foot-fetish buttons and gave him the perfect way to introduce me to the art of domination. It wasn't long before he'd
moved in with me.

When I came home, hot and tired after a long shift on my
feet behind the cupcake-bakery counter, Jason would offer to
massage my sweaty, stockinged feet. Of course, I never refused,
not when his fingers could so skillfully soothe away the aches
of the day. One night, thumbs working on the soft pad just
beneath my big toe, he made the casual comment, "Of course,
you should be demanding I do this as soon as you walk through
the door."

And that's how I came to spend my evenings on the couch,
Jason lying obediently on the floor while I rubbed my sweaty,
stockinged feet all over his face. Being made to do this got him
so hard his cock looked as though it might burst through the
tight-fitting Lycra of his shorts. His reward for licking and
sucking my nylon-clad soles was to be gently wanked between
my feet until his come spurted all over my stockings—at which
point, of course, he'd be ordered to clean them with his tongue.

"What would people think if they could see us?" Jason
would ask as he lay beneath my feet, naked from the waist down
and cock pointing rigidly toward me. "What would they say if
they walked in right now?" That was always the point where he
came. Simply expressing his desire to be caught in the act was
enough to tip him over the edge

I don't know when, if ever, Jason would have confessed on
his own that his love of foot worship was only the entrée to the
main course, that his desire to be humiliated and exposed ran
deeper than I could ever have suspected. I saved him the bother
by discovering his secret stash of porn.

Searching on the PC in the room Jason used as his home
office, looking for documents I needed to help me file my tax

return, I noticed a folder labeled CFNM. The initials sounded vaguely financial, so without thinking twice, I opened it. Inside, I found a collection of pictures and stories that told me everything I needed to know about dominating Jason. Clothed Female, Naked Male: I'd never heard the acronym until now, but here the fetish was, laid out in fantasy after fantasy. In every case a young man was manipulated into stripping bare for a group of older women who reveled in humiliating him just as much as he reveled in their cruel, clever treatment of him and their blatant admiration of his naked body.

I didn't know what was getting me wetter: the stories themselves, or the thought of Jason in that position, naked and at the mercy of his erotic tormentors. Of course, there was a chance this was one of those fantasies he had no intention of making reality, like the one I had about being fucked in the ass by the two cute builders renovating the flats across from the bakery, but there was an easy way to find out.

When I went downstairs, I took with me a basket full of dirty laundry. Jason was in the kitchen, pottering about in his workout gear.

"Those things look like they could do with a wash," I said. "Take them off and I'll pop them in with this load."

"Sure," he replied, "I'll just nip upstairs and change."

My tone was stern, the one I had, until now, reserved for our foot-fetish games. "Undress here. And don't think about putting anything else on."

Jason didn't need to speak the words, *You found them.* His expression right before he reached for the hem of his grubby T-shirt told me everything. In moments, he was standing naked, cock already starting its upward rise.

His eyes were downcast as he handed his discarded clothes to me. "Here you go, Ma'am." The deference in his voice was truly delicious. I would hear it over and again in the months to come.

But having him walk naked around the house, teasing him with the threat that one day he'd wake to find I'd locked all his clothes away and he'd only be allowed to dress when he went to work or out for the occasional drink with his friends, was one thing. Baring him in front of an appreciative female audience— which I quickly learned was the situation he longed for more than any other—was something else entirely. Until I thought of the perfect way to make it happen.

He finds me in the kitchen, hunting for the paper cocktail umbrellas I'm sure lurk in the back of a drawer. Hair still damp from the shower, wearing nothing but a towel knotted around his waist, he looks so fuckable I almost wish we could cancel tonight's little party.

"Not dressed yet?" I ask. "You know the girls will be here any moment."

"I just came down to get my shirt." He gestures to his favorite blue short-sleeved shirt, freshly ironed and waiting on a hanger for him. "Oh, and you haven't seen my flip-flops, have you?"

They're on the floor by the washing machine, lying where he kicked them off earlier, but I tell him, "Yeah, I think they're out by the back door."

"Thanks, Bev." He nips out into the backyard to find them. When the kitchen door closes behind him, I silently drop the latch. It takes him a minute or so to realize his flip-flops are nowhere to be seen, and when he tries the door, it quickly becomes obvious he can't get back inside.

"Hey, could you let me in please, babe?" he calls through the half-open window.

If he hasn't realized I've locked him out deliberately, or that

I'm gradually leading him into a predicament from which he can only escape on my terms, my next words make it clear. "Sure, Jason, but I want you to do something for me first. I want you to take your towel off and pass it through the window to me."

"Oh, Beverley. Sweetheart, no." His tone is despairing, but I wouldn't be at all surprised if his cock isn't tenting out the towel. Jason has never been outside with nothing on before, never been led out of his usual comfort zone, but I know he can't fail to be turned on at the thought.

"Come on, hand it over," I order him. "You don't still want to be naked when the girls get here, do you?"

His submissive heart must be telling him that's exactly what he wants, but his head says otherwise. I hear rustling noises, then the damp towel is being thrust toward me. I almost snatch it from Jason's hands and toss it into the washing machine.

When I glance out the window, I can see him in the fading light, skulking in the shadows by the high fence that separates us from next door. My clit is pulsing, nerves singing as I luxuriate in the knowledge that I've so skillfully contrived to make him strip bare for me, just like the men in his favorite fantasies. It's all I can do not to rub my pussy against the edge of the table in an attempt to scratch the itch.

If only he knew this was just the start.

"Okay, you can open the door now."

"What's wrong, Jason?" I ask. "Isn't this what you always wanted? To be outdoors, with not a stitch on, completely exposed…"

"Yes—god, yes." He groans. "But our guests…"

"Don't worry, darling. The patio doors are unlocked. You can let yourself in through those."

Briefly, he looks as though he might argue. Then the appeal of walking just that little distance in the nude becomes too much to resist. As he makes his way over to the patio, I dash into the living room to watch the show.

It obviously hasn't occurred to him in his horny but anxious state that it's dark enough for the security light to come on the moment he steps in range of the detectors. With the living room curtains pulled almost all the way across, the patio doors are framed like a stage. Jason's expression as the light illuminates his stark naked body—and, I can't help but notice, fully erect cock—is a thing of beauty. But it's not so much the fact he's so gorgeously showcased that alarms him as much as the realization that I'm not alone as I look out at him, grinning.

While he was in the shower, the girls arrived. For the last fifteen minutes, they've been sitting on the living room sofa as silently as they can, waiting for Jason to appear. I promised them a show they would never forget, but I don't think they believed I was serious. Now Liz and Sharon and Wendy sit, squealing in shock and delight, as Jason's hand drops to cup his cock and balls.

He reaches for the door handle, but I'm quicker. I open the door just a crack. "Now, now, Jason. Don't cover up that beautiful thing, not when the girls are so anxious to see it. Hands on your head, or I'll lock the door and leave you out there for a while."

Jason has no idea whether I'm serious about carrying out the threat. To be perfectly honest, neither do I. I've never thought of myself as cruel, but that was before I appreciated the power that comes from being fully clothed when the man you love is naked, helpless and willing to do whatever you say. Obviously not willing to take the risk, Jason grasps his hands together behind the back of his head.

Somewhere behind me, I hear Liz murmur, "I always reckoned he was big, but... Bev, you're such a lucky cow."

"I'll bring him in, so you can get a better look." The door pulled fully open, I usher Jason inside. Despite the embarrassment he must be feeling, his cock still juts up rigidly. "Turn around, Jason. Let them enjoy the back view, too."

Face blushing beet red, Jason does a slow circuit, so the ladies get to admire his pert asscheeks. I notice he didn't make any objections this time; simply did as he was told. He's submitting to me so beautifully, and the pulse between my legs beats even more strongly in response.

"I think the girls might like a drink now, Jason." What I really need is something to cool me down or, better yet, Jason's tongue lapping at the sticky furnace my pussy has become. If we were alone, I'd stop the game here and act on my need to be fucked, but I know Jason's need is to put on a performance for our guests. If that wasn't the case, he wouldn't have scuttled over to the table, wouldn't be pouring the mojitos into sugar-frosted glasses.

As he hands a glass to Liz, she asks him, "So how does it feel, to be completely bare when we're all sitting here fully clothed?"

He doesn't need to answer, not when his emotions are so clearly etched on his boyish face. We can all tell that to Jason, this feels right; that somehow it's the natural order of things to be naked and subservient in this situation.

"Oh, he's got to be enjoying it," Wendy chimes in. "Otherwise this wouldn't be so big and hard, would it, Jason?"

She reaches out and lazily trails her fingers along his shaft, all the way from base to tip, as though mentally filing its dimensions in her private wank bank, to bring out on those nights when she has only her rabbit vibrator for company. An unexpected pang of jealousy grips me, as Jason lets out a gentle hiss, taking pleasure from Wendy's touch. Then I tell myself this is what we both want, for Jason to be used as a plaything by someone other than me. After all, when the cocktails have been drunk, the nibbles devoured and the girls are on their way home, still not quite believing they've been allowed to touch and tease their naked manservant, I'll be the one who takes him upstairs and fucks him. Assuming we make it that far.

Now that the girls have realized they can touch as well as look, there's a moment when the evening threatens to descend into a free-for-all. Sharon grabs a handful of Jason's butt, squeezing hard, and I can't quite be sure, but it looks like Liz is playing with his balls. They're treating him as though he's just an object provided for their pleasure, and he's clearly loving it, but I can tell from the way he's breathing he's already on the fast track to orgasm, and the fun has barely begun.

Time to change tack, to offer him a slow, sustained torment that will keep him on the edge but not cause him to come just yet. "Ladies, help yourself to food," I suggest. It had been my intention to make Jason fill their plates, but I need to distract them long enough to let his arousal subside just a little, before we crank the pressure up again.

I settle back in my chair, poke a carrot stick into the pool of creamy dip and lick it off. Jason's eyes are fixed on the carrot as it disappears between my lips, going where his cock wishes so desperately to follow. *Not yet,* is my unspoken rebuke.

Liz sits down, sprawling back carelessly against the sofa cushions. In that position, she's giving Jason a perfect view of her panties, a tiny white triangle promising so much. Then she crosses her legs and that glimpse of heaven is blocked off.

Between us, we keep Jason on the edge for as long as we possibly can. Once in a while, I bring the conversation back to the fact that none of us has removed so much as a sandal, while Jason is completely naked. Every time I use words like "stripped" or "bare" to reinforce my point, he can't fail to react, body stiffening slightly. But the looks he flashes me tell me he's loving the way I've taken control.

The girls are playing their parts, too, idly stroking some area of his luscious, bare physique as he refills their glasses. Liz can barely keep away from his cock, while Wendy runs her hands over the firm ridges of his stomach. Jason has never endured so much buildup without release. It's only when Sharon glances at her watch and says, "I'll have to call a taxi, Bev. I told the babysitter I'd be back by ten," that I realize how much time has passed.

"That's fine," I tell her. "Jason just has one last thing to show you before you go."

Taxi ordered, Sharon can once more pay full attention as I launch into my speech.

"Now, I know you've enjoyed having a naked male to wait on you this evening, and I'm sure you're hoping for a repeat performance. Well, I don't know whether we're going to make this a regular event—" A quick glance across to Jason tells me a part of him would like that very much indeed, if only I will agree to it. "But what I do know is that Jason is more than ready to come. Do you think he deserves to?"

There's a general chorus of agreement that, yes, he's earned his orgasm. Liz is already shifting forward in her seat, no doubt hoping for the chance to play with him. But that's not how all the fantasies Jason reads and rereads come to their conclusion.

"More accurately, would you like to see him take hold of that huge, hard cock of his and wank it till he comes all over himself?"

"I'd love to," Wendy says. "We all would. But...won't that be embarrassing for him?"

My lips curve with barely suppressed amusement. "Darling, that's the whole point."

Further debate is unnecessary, if only because Jason has already grabbed his cock and is tugging at it with short, frantic strokes. If he's aware of four pairs of eyes watching his every movement, he doesn't say anything. He's already moving beyond shame, beyond the knowledge that tomorrow, or the day after, he'll bump into Liz or Sharon or Wendy in the gym and be reminded they've seen him perform this most intimate act. With his eyes half closed, his hand almost blurring on his shaft, I don't think I've ever seen Jason look so beautiful. Willingly making himself so vulnerable has only served to reveal his inner strength.

"Oh, god, Beverley, can't hold back." Jason sounds as though he's on the verge of sobbing, lost in a place where none of us can follow him. "Going to—going to..."

"That's it," Sharon urges. "Shoot your spunk." The words are so out of character for her, but her eyes are shining with lust and I'm sure her underwear is as soaked through as mine.

It's all the permission Jason needs. With a string of expletives, he surrenders to the inevitable, come oozing down over his fist. He slumps to his knees, drained. I can hear hooting, and I wonder who's congratulating him, then I realize Sharon's taxi has arrived and its impatient driver is sounding his horn in the street outside.

The party breaks up swiftly after that, the girls thanking me effusively for the most incredible evening. As soon as I've closed the door behind them, I pounce on Jason, devouring him with sloppy, rum-flavored kisses. Not only do we not make it as far as the bedroom, we don't even get out of the hall. Stripping off my saturated knickers, I push Jason to the floor and straddle his face. My skirt falls in loose folds around his head. It can't fail to remind him that I'm still clothed and he's still naked, just the way he likes it.

The moment his tongue makes contact with my clit, I know this is going to be fast and breathless and everything I need it to be. Grinding myself against his face, I savor the feeling of being on top, in every sense.

"So was tonight everything you'd hoped it would be?" I ask, rising up just enough to let Jason answer.

"God, yes. But next time, I want to be made to strip in front of them. Being naked when they saw me was amazing, but having to get naked for them would be even better."

"So you think there's going to be a next time, do you?"

"Will this help you say yes?" Jason's tongue returns to thrumming my clit, fast little flicks that make me think of a hummingbird's wings, beating and beating, hovering to stay still.

In the moment before my cunt seems to dissolve in liquid heat, I murmur, "Yes, Jason, we'll do this again. But only if you're very good."

"Oh, I will be, Ma'am," he promises me, and that's when I know what I've exposed tonight is only the beginning.

NEW GAMES ON A SATURDAY NIGHT

Teresa Noelle Roberts

Jack woke in the hot dark, roused from sleep by one of the various sounds of a Jamaica Plain side street in the middle of the night: the distant rumble of the Orange Line train, sirens on Centre Street, a barking dog across the street, a dull hum of conversation from outside—no words, just the sound of night-owl voices.

Or maybe it was the woman curled up next to him stirring in her dreams that woke him.

Woman next to him? What the...?

He jumped, then remembered why she was there.

Neither he nor the lady in question had planned to make this an overnight date. Sexy Serena with the very spankable heart-shaped ass had planned only to come back to his place after dinner and spend a few happy hours with him filling her long-standing fantasy about having that very spankable ass spanked. They'd been working up to this point for a while, with plenty of flirting and teasing mixed with some serious talks about the pleasures and dangers of bringing fantasies to life.

As an experienced top playing with a newbie bottom, Jack had figured it would be a fun couple of hours, he'd make sure Serena was all right, she'd take a cab home and either they'd get together down the road to explore further or they wouldn't. Just a little spanking and maybe some light bondage. Nothing more.

But that wasn't quite how it had gone. What he'd expected to be a lighthearted session that wouldn't exactly be a date had turned out to be far more intense—and far sexier—than he'd imagined.

It had been so long since he'd shared the thrill of a completely new game with someone sexually experienced but new to kink that he'd almost forgotten how hot it was. Serena had reminded him. A fairly mild spanking was…well, it was never dull to put a beautiful woman over his knee and turn her ass red, but he'd become accustomed to playmates who liked more exotic thrills. Single-tail whips. Play piercings. Being flogged while in inverted suspension bondage. With a lot of play buddies but no steady lover, coming up with new pleasure/pain challenges for his heavy-playing friends was part of the fun for him.

He'd almost forgotten how sensual it was to introduce someone to BDSM starting from scratch, to enjoy the simple pleasure of spanking a fine ass, to revel in her somewhat bewildered but eager enjoyment as stinging arousal built and crested. Serena might be inexperienced in terms of kink, but she was one sensuous, sexy and adventurous woman. The only reason they hadn't been up all night experimenting was that she'd been so aroused by the initial forays into spanking they'd fucked each other senseless and then passed out.

With so many wonderful things yet to do.

Another part of him woke up at that thought, stirred; suggested that he should move closer to her, caress her awake, kiss down her warm body to the heat between her legs and lick her until she added her own noises to those of the heated night. And once she was awake, aroused and ready, figure out which of many wonderful options to do next.

Hmm, that sounded like a good idea.

No, make that a great idea.

Even if the whole start-slow-and-sensuous technique wasn't normally his style. He considered himself a top-about-town, and his sexual encounters usually happened during or after play parties, where nipple clips and caning were the usual foreplay.

Then again, it had been a long time since he'd played with anyone who might appreciate a slower, more sensual buildup— a long time as in since his last serious relationship, which ended badly enough that he'd been happy, or to put it more honestly, safe, playing the field for the past several years. To his surprise, he realized he'd missed it.

Besides, it was fun to start slow, then work up to something wilder, then ramp down again. Did great things for a woman's mind, as well as her body.

That was his excuse if the dom-police came calling. But right now the truth was he just plain wanted to taste Serena.

He could barely see Serena's shape in the darkness, but Braille would work. He might not have her body memorized yet, but even though he was sure there were nooks and crannies aplenty still unexplored, erogenous zones still unaccounted for and, he hoped, kinks even she didn't know about yet to uncover, he could find the basics.

He pulled back the sheet, licked at a bead of sweat on her spine.

And came awake enough to realize why it was so hot, and why he could hear the neighborhood chorus instead of the familiar hum of central air.

Serena shivered at his caress, stretched and rolled over to face him. "Mmm, nice. Why's it so..." She mumbled something, and a switch apparently clicked in her brain. "Blackout or blown fuse?"

"No offense, but I hate you. You wake up much too coherent. I think blackout. Otherwise there'd be more light from outside." He yawned, ran his hand down her body, smiled even though she couldn't really see the smile. "Hey, I have an idea."

"I kind of figured that." She pressed herself against him, rubbing like a cat. "A big idea, I see."

His train of thought, which had been moving pretty erratically at best, almost got derailed by that. She felt so good against him, so hot.

But the vision in his head (sleepy as it was) was becoming a little more elaborate than just screwing Serena senseless in the dark bedroom, and it wouldn't let him go. "A very big idea. Too big for indoors. Come on." He got out of bed, although he swore the damp sheets were trying to hold on to him, and grabbed a few items from the bedside table.

Taking Serena's hand, he led her out of the bedroom, through the darkened kitchen, curiously quiet without that underlying appliance hum you didn't think about until it was gone. He took a key off a hook on the wall by the back door and then led her out. "Jack, I'm naked," she finally pointed out, tacking on, "We're naked," as if his bare ass might sway him where hers wouldn't.

"It's three in the morning and pitch dark. Besides, you're not naked. You're wearing a collar. Or you will be." He ran a narrow band of supple red leather over the curve of one glorious breast.

She drew in her breath on a sharp hiss. Her body curved forward, following the movement of the leather. Her eyes closed.

"Well, as long as I'm not completely naked, then it's all right."

"As long as you're wearing the collar, I want you to call me Sir. Can you do that for me, Serena?"

She giggled—nervously, he thought—but she opened her eyes very wide. "Part of me thinks that's silly," she admitted. "But part of me must think it's hot because I'm about ten times wetter."

Jack thought about his wording for a second before he answered, stroking Serena's heated skin as he thought. "It *is* silly if you look at it one way, like playing let's pretend as a kid. I'm not a knight by any stretch and while I guess you qualify as a damsel, you don't seem to be in distress." He trailed his fingers down her body, enjoying her squirmy reaction, and dipped them quickly between her legs. "Unless distress is a euphemism for *arousal*."

"That would certainly put a different spin on knights rescuing damsels in distress." Serena rolled her hips forward, seeking more from his questing fingers, but he pulled his hand back and used it to give her ass a quick, hard slap.

The flesh jiggled a bit under the blow. God, that sensation would never grow old.

She let out a surprised shriek. Then she sighed with pleasure as the sting softened into pleasure.

"So yeah, the 'Sir' thing is playing a game. But a fun game. A hot game. It's a way of saying you're putting yourself into my hands for a little while, like the collar. Pretending you're my slave or the damsel captured by the black knight or whatever."

She lifted her hair and let him fasten the collar. He wondered if she realized how she bowed her head as she did, or how beautiful she looked doing so.

"I like the idea," she whispered, "of putting myself into your hands for a while. I've always had a slave-girl fantasy."

His cock surged at the thought of Serena as his slave, under his command permanently. His cock didn't have a firm grasp on reality, he figured—putting a permanent collar on someone on the first date would be about as smart as proposing on the first date—but that didn't mean he couldn't enjoy the fantasy of owning this hot woman, as she would enjoy the fantasy of being owned.

And damn, she looked good in that collar.

He smacked her ass again. "Get moving before the power comes back on."

Two flights of stairs and they arrived. Jack used the key to open a stiff door and led Serena out onto the tiny roof deck. Serena must not have been able to see much in the darkness, but she looked around anyway, taking in what she could of small trees in big pots, planters full of flowers and vegetables, a clematis vine on a trellis. All the colors were faded to gray in the darkness, but maybe because of that, other senses seemed sharper. Scents of flowers, herbs and tomato plants hung thick in the air. They probably always did, but Jack rarely noticed them.

"It's beautiful," Serena breathed. "I like the city like this, all dark and almost quiet, and glowing in the distance where they still have power. And something smells like a cherry pie. Heliotrope?"

"Could be." Jack shrugged. "Mr. Figueroa and Kate take care of it. I throw money in to the plant fund so I can take tomatoes and herbs. The grill"—he pointed as if she could actually see the small charcoal-burning Weber in the dark far corner—"is mine."

"You cook?"

"I can't always find slave girls to do it for me."

A second's hesitation, and then Serena laughed. "And you

haven't found one this time, either. I'm a terrible cook."

"Don't you mean 'this time either, *Sir?*'" Jack gently touched the red collar still encircling her throat. "So forgetful—and so presumptuous." He hoped his tone was conveying how completely and utterly not upset he was. That didn't mean he might not punish her, or rather "punish" her with big air-quotes and a great deal of play melodrama, but he found the direct cheekiness refreshing.

She glanced away, clasped her hands behind her back as he'd instructed her earlier. Even in the darkness, he swore he could see her blush. "Sorry about that, Sir. It's not automatic yet. I expect that'll take a while." Her tone sounded just right to him: respectful, but not taking the whole thing too seriously, as if she knew it was a game. "As for cooking, seriously, you'd be better off at McDonald's. And I hate McDonald's."

"I can find better uses for you anyway."

The faint pearl of her skin in the dimness distracted him from distraction, reminded him that he hadn't gotten Serena out of bed just to talk, pleasant as the talking was. The collar cut a dark line against the pale skin of her throat. She was his for now, and it might be a game, but it was a delightful game, one he should definitely take advantage of. He reached around her from behind, pulled her back against him, loving the feel of her curves, the slightly damp heat of her skin. He ran one hand down her torso. Her skin twitched like a nervous racehorse, and she pushed back against him.

His hard-on had subsided as they'd chatted but he hardened almost instantly. He slipped his cock between her legs, rubbing along the slit that was already moistening, slicking up for him. She made a little choked noise, and Jack's cock jumped.

She was so excited already, and he hadn't even gotten started yet.

"Look up at the sky," Jack whispered into her ear. Her hair smelled like sex-sweat and rosemary.

"Stars. You can actually see stars tonight!" He felt rather than saw her smile. "I feel like I'm on vacation somewhere out of town."

She paused, then added quickly, "Sir," and he nodded approvingly, taking advantage of the fact she was looking away to grin like a kid in glee that she was getting into the spirit of the game so well.

"I'll see what I can do to make you see stars in the city as often as possible." While she gazed overhead, Jack fiddled with the small objects he'd palmed off the bedside table.

Pincher-style nipple clips, with a chain connecting them.

And she had the perfect breasts for them, neither tiny nor oversized, with plump, delicious nipples.

While she was distracted, he cupped her breast. She all but purred.

The metal had picked up the heat of his body as he held it, but the slickness of it elicited a puzzled noise from her as he drew it across her breast to her nipple. "Don't look," he whispered, putting all the authority he could muster into the soft tone.

He tightened it. Not too tight yet, just enough to pinch interestingly and let her feel the weight of it dangling from her nipple. If she liked that sensation, he'd tighten it more. Some women liked far stronger clamps on their nipples or ones with heavy weights attached to make the sensation more painful, more challenging. These clips didn't pinch as hard as determined fingers might, but they were steely and wouldn't let go and the very fact they weren't fingers made them interesting. "Now you can look."

An indrawn breath. "Wow," she said softly. "Wow...Sir."

Oh, yeah, that was what he liked to hear. He'd spent so long playing with women who knew exactly what they wanted he'd almost forgotten the way the sounds a woman made when she was on a voyage of discovery made him feel powerful.

And power surged directly to his cock—the power of administering a judicious taste of pain. It didn't have to be lots of pain, either. Sexy as it was to play with an experienced bottom who craved canes and single-tails and heavy paddles and wanted to end up looking like her ass and tits got run over by a bus, the turn-on wasn't so much giving the pain as being trusted to give just the right amount of pain.

And inexperienced Serena, who was still finding her own line between erotic pain and "Stop that now or I'm calling the cops," was showing him a tremendous amount of trust.

He clamped the other one into place, then tightened them farther.

She repeated, "Wow," her voice melting, somewhere between a gasp and a giggle. "That's...that's..." She shook her head, as if trying to jar the words loose. Her hair tickled his skin. "Amazing. I think I could go a little tighter, Sir."

With a grin, he complied. "Now lean forward and put your hands on the railing. It's good and sturdy."

Serena obeyed, sticking her ass out and wiggling it provocatively.

Not that he needed provocation.

Covered by the darkness and Serena's interest in her surroundings, he'd dropped the other objects he'd collected from the bedside table on a little round glass-topped table. Now, he groped until he found the leather slapper, a tongue-shaped sandwich of two pieces of thick burgundy leather with a handle of leather-wrapped hardwood.

He took a step backward, ran one hand over the inviting

moon of Serena's ass. God, it was gorgeous—heart shaped, well
padded, but proportional. Pale enough that it reddened nicely
and would show the results of his handiwork for a while. The
perfect female butt from the point of view of a dominant guy
who liked spanking.

He stroked a few more times, memorizing the contours. She
shivered. "It's a little tender, Sir," she said, her voice gleeful.
"And it feels really good."

"Tender? Excellent!" He pinched a spot that had been
a recipient of much attention earlier in the evening, and was
rewarded with a squeal, half indignant, half delighted.

The perfume of her arousal was mingling with the rich smell
of herbs, the honeyed flowers, the sharp smell of tomatoes, and
it was making him wild.

He stopped what he was doing and pressed his cock between
her legs, enjoying her slick heat on his hardness, teasing her clit
with the head of his cock. She writhed against him.

So tempting to push in now, to sheathe himself inside her
without further preliminaries. He knew she'd let him, and he'd
get the pleasure of feeling her body's slight resistance at first as
it tried to catch up with her mind's arousal, and then feel her
opening fully to him, getting slicker and wetter and more accom-
modating, then tightening again as he drove her to orgasm.

But he wouldn't. Not yet, no matter how tempting it was,
no matter how the memory of her sex gripping and clutching at
him earlier burned through him.

He had someplace he wanted to lead her first.

He'd promised her stars in the city. The studded sky above
the rooftop garden was pretty, but those weren't the stars he
meant.

Not the ones he figured she was craving. And certainly not
the ones he craved to give her.

Another pinch, this time on the spot. Then he drew his other hand back and delivered a swat with the slapper.

He knew this toy well, had tested it on himself when he first bought it and had used it on others often. The blow wasn't particularly hard; it should be pleasantly thumpy, with a little sting that others had described as delicious.

The *sound*, though, was astonishing: a loud, emphatic crack that seemed to echo in the quiet of the night.

She jumped, yelped, flinched away...

Then stuck her delightful butt out for more.

"Ask for it," he said. "Ask me nicely."

She caught her breath raggedly. "Please..."

"Please what?"

Did Serena have any idea that he was teasing himself with this game as much as he was her, pacing himself so he wouldn't overwhelm her adorable new submission by rushing through all the wonderful/evil things he wanted to do to her all at once? A woman just discovering the joys of the pleasure/pain edge was the shiniest toy a man like him could want.

Of course, he also felt that way when he played with an experienced bottom who knew exactly how she liked it and trusted him to deliver, and to push her outside her comfort zone in exciting ways. But something about Serena's eagerness and openness made everything as fresh for him as it was for her. Only his *everything* had a much larger scope than hers, at this point, so he had to be careful not to go too far too fast.

"Please, Sir."

There was pleading in the voice all right, but also a hint of mischief.

Oh, yeah. She was enjoying the game he played and was playing right back.

Luckily, that suited Jack's mood.

"Tell me what you want. Tell me what you want me to do to you."

This time she hesitated a little longer before begging, "Please, Sir, smack my ass again with that…" She hesitated. "That thing. That wonderful, awful thing."

Instead, he stroked the smooth skin gently, a lover's tender caress. "Are you sure?"

She pushed back against him. The "Yes!" was almost a sob.

"You didn't say Sir!" he said, marking each word with a quick, loud blow with the slapper. "Bad, bad, bad, naughty girl! You have to learn to say *Sir!*" All right, it wasn't Shakespeare, or even particularly sensible, but judging from Serena's reaction, he could have been speaking Swahili and it would have been all the same to her. The tone of voice was all that really mattered now, affectionate yet stern, guiding her through what she was feeling. He went on talking in much the same vein, telling her how naughty and wicked and lovely she was, as he slowed down the smacks while increasing their force.

Before long, she was keening, rolling her hips to take the blows at the best possible angle. He could hear the chain on the nipple clips clinking against the railing and knew that her movements were tugging at the clips, increasing the pleasurable pain.

How had he gotten so lucky? They'd met by chance through vanilla friends, neither of them looking for a new partner, but something had clicked. Showing this woman the joys of BDSM would be a delight. She was a natural—responsive, sexy, turned on by strong sensation, pain and authority—and seemingly unjaded, undamaged. Her fantasies might be dark, but she came to them fresh, almost innocent in some ways.

A few more thwacks and he stopped, ran his hand over an ass that seemed as steamy and heated as the asphalt had at midday.

Then he dipped his fingers between her legs and found her open, wanton, dripping.

"Now what should I do with you?" he mused, moving one finger in and out, barely inside the inviting lips, just enough to tease her. Tease them both, really. "Should I fuck you again?"

"Please, Sir!"

"You'd rather be fucked than paddled?" He tapped her inner thigh with the slapper. "Don't you like being paddled? Should I fuck you or paddle you?"

Serena shook her head wildly. The movement made her breasts bounce. The chains clinked against the railing and he knew the jouncing would tug on the clips, causing more delicious discomfort. "Don't know. I need...I want..." Her voice broke. Then she laughed a little hysterically. "Trick question, right? You decide, Sir. Either way I'll win. But if you can do both at once, that would be a double win."

He set the paddle down, picked up the familiar foil package next to it. "Clever girl. Clever girl who deserves a good fucking. Help me get this on, clever girl, and you'll get the fucking you deserve."

Four impatient hands got the condom in place.

He bent her over the railing again, pushed inside her as he'd been longing to do, pulled her hips back hard so her heated ass met his body with force.

"So hot," he murmured. "So wet. Such a hot, naughty, wonderful little slut." He was guessing on the *slut*; he hadn't thought to ask Serena if she liked that kind of dirty talk.

Apparently she did.

She made a funny little noise and rippled around him, sending shudders of delight radiating from his cock throughout his body.

Sweet. So sweet.

"That's my good little slut. You like it when I call you that, don't you?" Okay, it was self-evident that she did, so it was a silly thing to say, but Jack doubted Serena was feeling overly analytical at this point. (If she was, he was doing something wrong.)

"Yes, Sir," she gasped out between clenched teeth. "Oh, yes." The second yes was said on a hiss. She arched, pushing her hips back and up, her breasts down. The fine chain between the nipple clamps clinked delicately, adding to the symphony of ragged breath and flesh against flesh and the wet music of cock in cunt.

The clips...oh, yes, mustn't forget those.

Jack moved his hands, sliding them along her sweat-sleeked curves from hips to breasts. He ran his thumbs over her nipples and was rewarded with a wild-animal noise and a bucking motion that suggested Serena was on the edge of orgasm.

"Time to take these off," he whispered in her ear. "You let me know when you're going to come and I'll take them off then. You understand?" It was an effort to keep talking so coherently, but that wasn't a bad thing. It kept him focused. Kept him from rushing, from exploding inside her before they were both ready.

Serena didn't answer right away. "Do you understand?" He thrust into her hard, making it punctuation.

Then he grabbed up the slapper again and applied it to her thigh.

This time, her "Yes!" was not just a response to the question. She rolled her hips, and he felt her body shuddering. He didn't need to hear her "Gonna come, Sir" to know it.

He eased the nipple clips off her, wondering as he did whether she realized that this was the moment they gave the most intense sensation—not going on, but coming off.

Serena let out a howl, part pain, yet all pleasure. The silk walls of her sex clamped down on him hard as she spasmed.

He'd meant to draw it out longer, but damn, she felt too sweet around him, too tight and hot and passionate, and with the noise she was making and the wonderful way she was rolling her hips and how crazy-proud it made him that she was taking everything so beautifully, like she was born to it, there was only so much a man could take. "My...sweet...slutty...girl," he grunted as he exploded inside her.

As soon as his brain recongealed, he panicked a bit, remembering the possessive words, the possessive tone. The possessive way he'd felt at that second, as if he'd won some kind of lust lottery and Serena was his grand prize.

He was so not ready for that, he told himself firmly—but he figured he'd earned feeling that way for a few blissful seconds.

That illusion was part of the game, like the collar and the *Sir* and the pretense that he was punishing her when it was something they both craved.

Unless he got really lucky and the sense that she was his, and maybe that a little bit of him was hers, stopped being a game and became truth. It hadn't worked the last time he'd thought that... but maybe it was about time he allowed himself to consider that possibility again.

He wasn't going to hold his breath that after years of happily playing with friends and not even looking for a full-time sub, he'd chanced to meet someone who might become more. But a guy, drunk on hormones and games on a summer night with a beautiful kinky woman, could dream.

And if the dream led to more pain for him than he'd ever cause her?

Right now it seemed worth it.

NOTES FROM HER MASTER

Kathleen Tudor

M aster led me through the crowd by the hand—our substitute when leashes are less than practical. His commanding jerks on my wrist guided me along behind him as he drove himself forward. Master has a sense of command about him that even people who are not into power exchange can feel, so he easily cleared a path to the security checkpoint at the airport.

When he stopped moving and gave one more sharp tug on my arm, I moved to a heel position, my eyes properly downcast. He came to stand in front of me and placed a box in my hand. "A little gift for you. You may open it once the plane takes off. Understand, Pet?" I nodded, pleased to note through my lashes that the corners of his mouth were turned up in pleasure.

"Good girl," he whispered. "Look up." I smiled as I was allowed the reward of looking him full in the face. "You're wearing your chastity belt?" I nodded. He didn't really have to ask, but it was our ritual. "You've provided me with your full hotel contact information and your itinerary?" Another nod.

"Very good." From his pocket he pulled a small piece of candy and fed it to me as a reward. I smiled again. "Now put on your business face. Have a good trip." He kissed me, using the opportunity to pinch my nipple hard enough to make my eyes water, and stepped back to let me go through security.

Our ritual was always the same. Because I love to work and he doesn't, Master allowed me to keep my job after I was collared. I provide for his needs during the day by working, and am ready to serve him from the moment I return. When I have to go away on business, I have a very strict protocol to follow.

My chastity belt must be in place before I leave home, and the key must be in his possession. I must provide him with an itinerary in minute detail, including travel time. If I am not at a business function, I must be in my hotel room as soon as possible, where I can order food up. I love how he keeps his hold over me no matter where I am.

Despite leaving my Master for three days, I was in a wonderful mood as I stepped onto the plane to find my seat. The box was on my lap, and I toyed with it as I waited for the plane to finish boarding, eager to see what was hidden inside. As I fiddled and mused, staring out the window to watch them load the luggage, I felt a presence beside me and glanced over. I smiled when I saw a colleague, Robert.

"Hi, Robert, how are you?"

"Pretty good. I'm heading to a conference. You, too?"

I agreed and we chatted for a while until the plane began to taxi. Robert laid a blanket over his lap, leaned back and put on some headphones, and I laid my eager hands on the box to wait another few moments. At last we were in the air. To be safe, I waited until we leveled out before I opened the small box and pulled out a PDA. A note on the back said, *Turn it on. M.* I turned it on, but nothing happened. Since I hadn't been told to do anything else with it, I set it in my lap and picked up a magazine to read.

We were fifteen minutes into the five-hour flight when the alarm on the PDA startled me. Robert, who looked like he had been sleeping, opened one eye and grinned at me. I grinned sheepishly and peeked at the screen. It had the alarm message displayed with a note below it: *Set PDA to VIBRATE. Undo three buttons. M.* My blouse was buttoned up to my chin, but three buttons brought it well down into my cleavage. I flushed as I followed the command, hoping that Robert wouldn't notice.

It took fifteen minutes before I began to feel relaxed again. That feeling ended when a silent buzz against my leg had me looking at the PDA screen once more. Obviously Master had a game going, but he couldn't have realized that a colleague would be my seatmate. I took a deep breath as I read: *Find the note in the front pocket of your carry-on. M.* The note was easy to find, folded twice in a straightforward, masculine way. Master's handwriting was blocky on the page. *Hello, Pet. Do you miss me, yet? Perhaps we should alleviate that. Close your eyes, my girl, spread your legs, and enjoy the feel of those soft thighs for me. You can even pretend I'm right there. M.* It went on below that: *P.S. You may need to lift your skirt some to get the full experience...*

Shaking, I glanced over at Robert. His eyes were still shut. Master hadn't said I had to be uncovered, so I shook out my blanket, spread my legs, and started to let my fingers drift. I had barely started when the PDA buzzed again. *Remove whatever you're covering up with. M.* Tears started to sting my eyes at the fear of being caught by Robert. His eyes were closed, though, and he hadn't stirred since the first alarm chimed. I pressed my eyes so tightly shut that it hurt, pushed the blanket to the floor, and let my fingers continue to trace my thighs. The pleasure was almost nullified by the fear, but the sheer danger of being caught lit my inner fires.

Breath shallow, I continued to stroke myself for ten minutes before the alarm buzzed against my leg again. I snatched at it, fearful, excited and unsure. *Take a break. After the peanuts, check page forty-four of your book. M.* Righting my clothing, I snatched the blanket back onto my lap as if to hide what had already been done. The timing was perfect; I had just become somewhat less flushed and warm when the stewardess came by and offered a snack and a drink. I declined the drink, and was almost giddy when I saw that our snacks were not peanuts, but pretzels. At least he didn't know *everything.*

I enjoyed the salty snack then dove into my bag for the book I had brought. There was indeed a small piece of paper tucked between the pages. *I'm sure you're doing lovely, Pet. Good girl. It must be hard for you to be so embarrassed. Still, a good Master must be firm. If there is a man nearby, he must be rather firm as well, don't you think? A good girl would offer a hand. M.* My face must have been cherry red to the hairline as I glanced at Robert out of the corner of my eye. There was in fact a bulge appearing underneath his lap blanket, and his eyes, I noticed, were not fully closed. He had been watching me.

My heart was pounding. Master could not possibly have known that I would be sitting beside a colleague. This could ruin my career. On the other hand, Master was the one who had allowed me to have a career in the first place. When I agreed to be his slave and wear his collar, I promised obedience in all things. Was my career more important than that promise? My hand found the band of silver tight around my neck, and I turned to look full on at Robert.

"Oh, Robert, I'm so sorry. I thought that you were asleep." I took a deep breath and swallowed hard. "It looks like I've caused you some, uh, discomfort. Can I, um, can I give you a hand with that?" I could barely breathe. Robert's eyes widened, then he reached to put the armrest in between us up and out of the way.

"Go ahead."

I reached across the seat, having to lean a little over his lap to get a good grip on his cock. To my surprise, it was already free of his slacks, pushing proudly up to form the bulge that I had seen. His cock was warm in my hand, and pleasantly thick. I immediately started in with the tricks that I knew made Master come the fastest, but Robert bent forward slightly to whisper in my ear, "Nice and slow, baby." He shifted to lean back a little in his seat, smiling as he held a magazine in one hand to cover what was going on in his lap. His precome dripped freely, and the sticky semen coated my fingertips.

My PDA buzzed, and I glanced behind me, unsure if I should check it out before I was done. "Go ahead, get it," Robert said, and I obeyed.

Page sixty-two, Pet. M. I opened my book again, and sure enough, another small piece of paper was tucked inside. *If your seatmate is done, you may cease. Otherwise, perhaps you should take him to the bathroom and offer him that sweet mouth of yours. And if that is the case, perhaps you need to brush up on these skills? You will obey his wishes. M.*

I put the piece of paper down, and Robert raised his eyebrows in question. "Just a reminder," I said. "Um, you're still...I mean...uh, maybe you'd rather me use some other skills?" I licked my lips, and understanding dawned on his face. He quickly arranged things under the blanket, then stood up to walk to the bathroom. I followed.

We squeezed into the tiny stall when no one was looking, and Robert leaned back, sitting on the lid of the little toilet and baring his cock for me again. I licked my lips as I knelt in front of him, looking up at him from between his knees. "Go on, then, do it," he said, and I leaned forward to swallow his cock.

He smelled like soap as I took his entire length in my mouth, allowing his cock to slide down my throat as I had practiced, burying my nose in his pubic hair. He remained quiet, only panting above me as I swallowed twice then began to bob up and down his shaft. My tongue worked the length of his cock, dancing and teasing as it had been trained to do. Blow jobs are an art form, Master always said, and I had been taught to be a master of that art. Despite my earlier attentions, Robert managed to hold out as I fucked him with my tongue, lips and throat.

His hand was on the back of my head as I rode him with my face. "Do you know what I've wanted to do since we met?" I indicated that I didn't. "This." His gentle hand turned into a rough fist tangling in my hair. He stood up, forcing me to bend back at an odd angle in the confined space. I couldn't move at all as he drove himself hard into my throat. I relaxed, fighting the urge to resist, which would make me gag. He slowed, teasing himself with long, slow strokes before ramming into my throat again. Tears spilled down my cheeks as I licked and sucked to add to his pleasure.

As suddenly as it had all started, Robert pulled away and dragged me to my feet by my hair. "You're just no good at that, are you?" he asked, and tears of anger and shame burned their way down my cheeks as I averted my eyes. He placed a hand down low on my leg, almost at my knee. "Your mascara's running, babe. I like that look." His hand traveled slowly up my leg, reaching my slick juices only halfway up. "Seems like you like it too, huh?" I bit my lip in silence, wondering why my Master would command this. Then again, how could he have predicted it? I knew that with my chastity belt, at least that part of me was safe.

His eyes went wide as he reached the metal that protected my dripping, throbbing cunt. "Poor girl, all horny and locked away. Take it off."

"I can't," I said. "I don't have a key." He slapped me with his right hand, and as my head swung to the side, I saw the key that he was holding in his left.

"I *said* to take it off."

Oh, god, Master knew. Robert was in on it. Oh, god! The belt was clinking into the sink almost before I knew I had reached for the key, and my eyes stared up hungrily at Robert. This was what Master wanted, and I was more than ready to oblige. My cunt was hungry for him as I reached for his cock.

He surprised me when he grabbed me, spinning me around and pushing me forward just slowly enough that I could catch myself on the door without making noise. My skirt flew up over my hips, and I bit down to keep from crying out as he penetrated me.

He thrust deep, pounding into me. "Touch yourself," he whispered, and I reached forward to oblige, his thick cock and my own fingers flying over my clit driving me toward orgasm like a train on a track. I came hard and fast, clenching around him and driving him over the edge with me.

Robert came with a groan that was muffled by the skin of my back as he bit down, hard. We both took a moment, panting, then he pulled out, wiped himself off, and pulled his slacks up again. He held my arms as he helped me switch places with him, then took a long look up and down my body. "You look like a damn slut. Clean yourself up."

"Yes, Sir," I whispered, locking the door behind him as he returned to his seat. I looked in the mirror. I *did* look like a slut, and a very satisfied one at that. My fingers were still shaky as I pulled my belt back into place. Robert had taken the key back. I scrubbed my face, straightened my clothes, and then went back to sit beside Robert. My PDA was flashing.

I looked at the message on the screen. *Page three hundred. Good girl. M.* The last note was in the same strong handwriting. *You may discuss today with Robert if you wish. I trust that you were a good girl and that you served him well. Your room will be shared. Tell him that I trust he will enjoy my hospitality for the duration of the conference trip. M.* I showed the note to Robert, and his smile—no less than feral—was enough to start my fires burning all over again.

LAP IT UP

Kay Jaybee

That's my last one." Louise stroked the puppy softly on the top of his chocolate-brown head, placed the dish of food beneath his eager mouth, bolted the recovery cage door and walked toward her colleague.

Jo was scribbling notes onto a medical chart that hung from a similar cage, "Yep, I'm done too." Giving her canine patient a final check, she accompanied Louise to the far corner of the veterinary clinic's hospital wing.

Ascending a short flight of stairs leading to the converted attic that served as the sleeping quarters for the animal-care nurses on night duty, both women squeezed past open boxes of pet food and equipment, semi-open packets of cleaning equipment, medical gloves and operating robes.

"I'm exhausted," Louise said, collapsing against one of the single camp beds and kicking off her shoes as she glanced at her watch. "It's almost midnight already."

Jo perched on the edge of the neighboring bed, grinning suggestively. "Are you really too tired?"

Lifting herself up onto her elbows, a faint smile hovered at the corner of Louise's lips. "You're unstoppable! Where do you get your energy from?"

"Well, seeing you in that outfit helps."

"But it's the same as yours!" Louise stared down at her veterinary nurse uniform, a bottle-green tunic that strained a little over her substantial chest, and practical, rather unflattering, black trousers, "How can you possibly find it a turn-on?"

"For one thing, you're wearing it." Jo got up and sat behind Louise, wrapping her arms around her lover's waist. "And for another thing, I know exactly how fantastic you look beneath it."

Shifting herself so she was leaning against her companion, feeling the heat of Jo's body radiating through her back, Louise replied, "You're not so bad yourself, honey." Twisting her neck around, she kissed Jo gently on her lipstick-free mouth.

Responding with increasing pressure, Jo tugged Louise's tunic open and ran a palm over the white cotton bra beneath, enjoying the pressure of a taut nipple as it pushed against the material restraint.

Louise, trapped under Jo, tried to lean forward to reciprocate the move, but found her hand slapped away. "Oh no, sweetie," Jo murmured into Louise's ear, "I have other plans for you tonight." Sitting up, her legs straddled over Louise's waist, Jo grasped her lover's wrists. "Fancy trying something different?"

"Such as?" Louise peered up at Jo through her fringe of blonde hair, her curiosity as intense as her arousal.

"I've had this fantasy going around my head for a while. Will you play with me?"

Louise looked wary for a second. Jo's fantasies generally headed toward some level of domination. The question was, how dominant?

Trailing a single finger around the edge of Louise's bra, Jo teased the soft pale skin that poked tantalizingly out of its low-cut cups. Flutters of erotic tension began to ignite the nerves in Louise's tits, flooding sparks of lust through her curvaceous body, making it all too easy to give in to any demand Jo might make of her. "How could I possibly refuse?"

Smiling briefly at her success, Jo's expression quickly became stern as she gripped Louise's wrists tighter and dragged her up so they sat only inches from each other, face-to-face. Her voice took on a commanding, no-nonsense tone. "I happen to know that your favorite sensation in the whole wide world is to feel a tongue between your legs."

Louise grinned. "Can't argue with that."

"If you do what I say, that will be your reward. But you have to do *everything* that I say. You will not speak, for bitches like you do not speak. In fact, bitches like you, with your long golden coat and your panting hungry mouth, *can't* speak."

Realization dawning as to the nature of Jo's latest game, Louise nodded, her body tensing at the idea of the pleasure to come. A pleasure that would only be reached, she suspected, after a certain level of discomfort.

Jo, confident that Louise would not move unless instructed otherwise, stood up. "Off the bed. Dogs have no place on the furniture."

Louise leapt down instantly. Unsure whether to stand or fall onto all fours, she adopted middle ground, bowing at her mock-mistress's feet.

The glare on Jo's face told her she'd chosen wrong, and Louise hastily repositioned herself onto her knees and elbows, her head hanging down like a puppy that knows it's done wrong, but doesn't really understand why.

"Stay!" Jo directed the order at Louise before walking away

and rummaging through the boxes of stock that cluttered the other end of the room.

The drumming of Louise's heart began to thud in her ears as well as her breast. All manner of things were hidden amongst the mess of animal-care supplies, and she couldn't stop her imagination from skipping ahead to some of the items Jo might find, and what use she might put them to.

Her tunic flapped open as she waited, and her trousers, which were a snug fit at the best of times, started to dig into her. Louise could feel the dampness that had started to leak from her pussy smear against her knickers as she waited for something to happen.

Jo returned, dropping her unseen prize on the bed. It was clear from the look on her face that she was pleased with whatever she'd found. Louise's muscles tensed further in anticipation of the pain she was sure was about to come.

She was taken by surprise, however, when Jo knelt next to her and began to gently ruffle her long golden locks, untying them from her topknot ponytail, letting it hang down her head and neck. As if pampering a treasured pet, Jo smoothed and stroked Louise, moving from her sleek golden hair to her back and beyond, paying particular attention to the rounded curves of her ass through the stretched fabric of her trousers.

Finding it difficult to remain still, Louise shuffled slightly toward Jo's crouched frame. The effect of her infraction was immediate. Her mistress moved away, standing so she towered above Louise, an expression of disapproval etched upon her pale features, her brown hair framing her cross face. "I believe you were told not to move!"

"Sorry," Louise mumbled as she stared at the floor.

"I also told you not to speak!"

The sound of a firm smack echoed around the room as it

rebounded off Louise's prone backside, making her whine with the sharpness of the pain.

"You may well whine like the bitch you are." Jo followed up the first slap with a second, which stung Louise despite the padding of her trousers and knickers. "Perhaps you don't want your reward, after all?"

Biting back the desire to cry out that she wanted the licking she was due right now, and doing her best not to flinch further, Louise withstood two more strikes before Jo stopped the punishment and resumed her tender cosseting. This time however, Jo combined the stroking with the slow removal of her temporary pet's uniform, giving permission where necessary for her to sit or stand in order to make the stripping easier to achieve.

Naked, and back on all fours, Louise's ample tits hung down invitingly, tempting Jo. But she was determined to continue with her fantasy, and so resisted the craving to suckle her lover's gorgeous cream tits. Instead she instructed Louise to watch while she took off her own clothes, revealing a deliciously sexy maroon lace bra, some ultra-brief knickers and incredibly sheer black stockings.

The "Wow!" that escaped from Louise's unbidden lips went unpunished, as Jo swelled beneath the wide-eyed appreciation of her girl. With hands on her hips, her face set in determination, Jo took a brand-new dog collar and secured it around Louise's statue-still neck. Then, fixing a matching lead in place, Jo ordered, "Heel," and began to walk her fantasy dog around the small area of room that remained clutter free.

Louise's bare knees and palms rubbed and scratched against the poorly carpeted floor as she struggled to match Jo's long stride and fast pace. The stiff leather collar cut into her neck as the lead was yanked sharply each time she failed to keep up with her mistress on their circuits of the confined space, a voice in the back of her head telling her it would be worth it to feel Jo's tongue against her clit. A thought she regretted, as even the idea of the expertly applied intimate stimulation sent fresh ripples through her chest, and shock waves of longing to her pussy.

After five dizzying turns of the room, Jo halted and held up her hand to Louise, giving the canine order to sit. She nodded approvingly as Louise promptly fell back onto her haunches.

"Over!" Jo commanded. Louise obliged, dropping to the floor and rolling onto her back.

Kneeling, Jo began to rub Louise's stomach as if praising her, then without warning, she flicked a single finger between her open legs, making Louise draw in a sharp breath.

"You are one wet bitch." Jo's eyes shone as she spoke. "Would you like me to lick my doggy better?"

Louise nodded emphatically.

"So, my little pup thinks she's earned the right to have me lap between her legs already, does she?"

Louise nodded again, but more warily than before, clenching her teeth together to prevent herself from making a sound.

"Well, that will all depend on how well you carry out the next few tasks, won't it?" Jo gestured with her hands again, and Louise repositioned herself onto all fours, her breasts hanging down invitingly once more. This time Jo could not resist, and crawled beneath her girl, repeating her warning—"You will not move, you will not make a sound"—before sucking at the right teat.

Louise closed her eyes, lost in a taut bliss that shot through her body as her sensitive nipple was licked to distraction. Stopping only to swap sides, Jo kept up the wonderful attention, reveling in the taste and texture of her partner.

Finally having had her fill of the luscious globes, Jo withdrew and moved to look at Louise's face, which was creased with a combination of lust and deep concentration. Jo's body gave an involuntary shiver of longing as she considered what she was about to do next. Aware that her own arousal was rapidly growing, she decided it was time to lose the last layer of her clothing and peeled off her underwear before her rapt audience.

Louise couldn't help reacting as her lover's body was revealed, but mindful of her position, she managed to turn her sigh of appreciation into a long, dog-like pant. Her arms were beginning to ache at having to support her weight, and Louise knew she was going to have to move again soon, or she'd collapse onto the rough floor.

As if reading her pet's needs, Jo spoke. "You'd better ask me nicely, if you want to move."

"Please can I…"

The smack across her hindquarters bought Louise's sentence to a premature end. How was she supposed to ask to move if she couldn't speak? She paused for a second, then gingerly picking up the hanging lead in her teeth, Louise rose onto her back legs, acting like a dog wanting to go for a walk.

"Good girl." Jo tousled Louise's hair. "Let's go." She took the lead from Louise's mouth, and took her on another circuit of their attic room.

Returning to the foot of Louise's bed, Jo let go of the lead and allowed her bitch to lie on the floor. Leaving Louise on the ground resting her weary limbs, Jo returned to the pile of stock to search for the next item she required. "Now, I seem to remember you wanted a good licking."

Louise whimpered, widening her eyes like a begging dog.

"Well then, if you can lap up all the water in this bowl, without spilling a single drop, then, in return, I will lick and kiss your gorgeous sweet pussy until you howl like a hound."

Jo flashed a large silver dog bowl in front of Louise, then took it over to the sink in the corner of the room and filled it to the brim. Moving slowly, so that none of liquid spilled, Jo placed the bowl before Louise and ordered her back to all fours.

The amount of water contained within the bowl looked almost impossible to lap up to Louise, and she gazed up at Jo questioningly for a second.

"Well, if you don't want to feel this tongue between your hind legs, doggie, then that's fine, I'll just sort myself out and leave you in peace." Jo opened her legs wide and began to stroke a finger teasingly over her own clit.

Louise felt irrationally jealous of that finger as it caressed Jo where she badly wanted to be caressed herself. The promise of her lover's expert tongue over her own nub was too much. Even if she ended up dribbling the contents everywhere, she had to try, however humiliating. She'd already walked on a lead and begged like a dog; what did it matter now?

Lowering her head to the bowl, Louise stuck her tongue out gingerly, and after doing her best to flick her hair out of the way without the use of her hands, began to lick at the ice-cold water. It was surprisingly easy to consume a small mouthful of liquid at a time, but it was incredibly difficult to do so without spraying drips of fluid over the edges of the bowl.

Squatting down to observe Louise closely, Jo spanked her willing victim's exposed rump each time the tiniest trickle of water escaped from the sides of the container. With every beautifully warming strike of her backside, Louise had to concentrate harder and harder not to choke, and consequently slopped even more water onto the now-wet carpet.

Abandoning all thoughts of trying to stop the bowl from overflowing, Louise sped up her lapping. Rolling her tongue like a scoop, she gulped the drink faster and faster, until it dripped from her nose, cheeks and chin. Her knotted hair dangled in the puddles that were forming around the outside of the bowl. The spanking of her ass came more rapidly now, and Louise's whole frame began to shiver and ripple with signs of her fast-climbing climax, as Jo combined a jabbing finger against the entrance to her anus with each corresponding smack. The relentless burning smacks no longer had any connection to the spatters Louise was throwing from the bowl.

Panting and gasping for air, Louise lapped so fiercely at the bowl that she accidentally tipped it over with her chin, sending the remaining fluid streaking across the bedroom floor in a small stream. Nervously, but with undeniable excitement, Louise glanced at her mistress.

"You bad dog! Look at the mess you've made. I should make you lick every drop up off the floor!"

Louise lowered her eyes sheepishly, like a chastised animal, and waited for a slap.

It didn't come. Jo, her body high on the power she held over her girl, couldn't wait any longer to taste Louise's slick juices. With a supreme effort, she managed to keep up her dominant stance. "Lie in your own mess. Go on! Get on your back, bitch."

Louise rolled swiftly onto her back once more, the water squelching beneath her sweat-soaked skin, the thin sodden carpet irritating her sore, red-blotched backside.

"No way do you deserve this," said Jo as she fell to her knees, "but I do, so I'm going to do it anyway."

Putting a gentle tongue to Louise's clit, Jo smiled to herself as Louise whimpered in heartfelt satisfaction, the flutters of her orgasm sending quivers of desire across her exhausted body. "Now this, my pretty little bitch, is the best way to lap it up, don't you think?"

The little bitch in question groaned out a prolonged, deep and relieved bark, in total agreement with her beloved mistress.

WHAT IF

Angela R. Sargenti

W hat if I pushed my boobs together so you could fuck my tits?" she asked me.

"What if I tossed your salad?"

"What if I put on a strap-on and showed you what it's like to take it in the ass?"

This was our favorite game. We'd say these things to each other until we hit on the perfect way to occupy our time for the night, and tonight was no different.

"What if I tied you up and teased you to tears?" I asked.

"What if...no, wait," she said. "That actually sounds pretty fun."

"Let's go."

A short time later, she was naked and bound facedown to our bed and I was working the feather tickler. I had her blind-folded to heighten the suspense, and just for fun I reached out and smacked her ass.

She moaned and stirred, helpless in her bonds. I wanted to

fuck her right then, wanted to climb right on top of her and take her in the ass.

Instead, I grabbed a ballpoint pen from the nightstand and retracted the cartridge, using it to trace the pink outline of my handprint.

"Oh, my god, what is that?"

"I'm not telling."

I slapped a pink mark on her other cheek, but this time I traced it with my tongue. She squirmed around, anxious for me to touch her, but what I did instead was, I took the tickler and turned it around to touch her cunt lips with the handle. She tried to wriggle closer, but I pulled it away.

She made a frustrated noise that made me smile.

"How long will it take for me to drive you crazy?" I wondered aloud. I slipped off the gold chain around my neck—the one she'd given me—and I let the cold metal dangle between her legs.

"You're already driving me crazy," she told me.

"But you said to tears."

"Oh, yeah."

I snatched the chain back and laid it aside. I took off my T-shirt next and fanned it over her a couple of times, and then I flicked it all over her body, down her legs, her arms, even over her ass. I didn't do it hard or anything, just enough to make her aware of it, and as suddenly as I began, I stopped.

I stood there motionless, not making a sound.

All I could hear was the ticking of the clock, and with each tick, the tension grew. But I was having a lot of fun and I wasn't ready to end it so soon, so I broke the suspense for her.

"Stay here a sec," I told her. "I have to get a few things."

It spoke to the bond of trust we'd built up during our relationship that she didn't protest, and when I got back from the kitchen, she was still waiting patiently.

"Now," I told her, "now you have to guess what you feel."

I scraped a dry sponge down her back, but she couldn't guess what it was. Next, I took a handful of spaghetti noodles, holding them like a whisk broom while I brushed them up and down her calves.

She didn't figure that one out, either, but she guessed the next few things with ease. One was a Q-tip I used to prod each of her fingertips until she laughed. The next thing was a blank CD I lay on her bare ass. I brushed a pastry brush up her thighs and tickled her feet with a clean dishcloth, but she let out a squeal when I dribbled chilled wine into the little dent at the small of her back.

"Oh, here," I said, bending down to lap it up with my tongue. "Let me get that."

I meant to only clean her up, but once I was down there, I smelled her arousal and spread her asscheeks apart with one hand to lay a finger on the cute little bud of an asshole I exposed. I delved down and dipped into her pussy as far as my finger would go, then I returned to coat her perfect asshole with her own sweet juices.

She strained toward me, not caring which hole I penetrated, but I didn't do either.

I moved away and found the next object.

I play-spanked her with the wooden spoon a couple of times and told her what a naughty girl she was, then I flipped it around and used the handle to gently prod her. I poked her bottom and her thighs and the side of one breast, never getting close enough to either one of her openings to satisfy her. She wriggled around a little and I snaked a hand up under her and tweaked her nipple.

I pulled out my hand and used it to pet her pussy a little,

once going so far as to almost dip my finger back in.

Almost.

When I moved my hand away, she murmured a protest.

"That wasn't a sob, was it?" I teased.

"Hell, no."

"Good. We still have a long way to go."

She let out a frustrated sigh, but she settled herself in for some more.

I dribbled dry beans on her back and plucked at her cute little butt with a pair of chopsticks. I rolled a cold tangerine down her spine and used a rolling pin to relax the muscles in her legs, then I smacked her ass lightly a few times with a rubber spatula. A salad fork made for a nice back-scratcher, and the handle of the lemon reamer a wonderful substitute for a butt plug.

She startled when I popped open the can of biscuits, then sucked in a breath when I laid the two first cold pieces of raw dough on her shoulders. A marble followed the tangerine down the slope of her back, then I ripped open a single-serve packet of honey and squirted it on her behind.

I swiped a little of it up with my fingers and brought it to her mouth. She licked off the bulk of it, then she made my cock twitch by sucking the rest off.

"What if I just left you there like that for, say, twenty minutes?"

"No!"

"Okay," I grinned, probing her some more with the wooden spoon.

She had to give in soon or I would, so I stuffed some corks between her toes and licked the rest of the honey off her ass. That almost did her in, but I kept on, dragging my tongue up her spine.

She groaned in shuddering agony and tested her bonds.

"What if I told you to open your mouth?"

She did what I asked and stuck her own tongue out, and I sprayed some canned whipped cream on it and let her taste it.

Now I teased her with my words, too, drawing tight little circles around her entrance with my forefinger and letting it brush her clit about every third pass. She tried to impale herself again, but I wouldn't hear of it.

"What if I just did this all day? What if I teased you all day long?"

"What if I screamed?" she asked, wiggling around on the sheet to find some way to pleasure herself and ease her throbbing clit.

"Does my pretty little baby want some dick?"

"Yes."

"Yes, what?"

"Please?"

I landed two more smacks with the rubber spatula and told her no.

She was real close to breaking now and I pumped my finger into her a few brief times, still avoiding her clit.

"What if I tickled you right here with this feather thing for a while?"

"Come on," she whispered urgently.

I chuckled softly.

"This will stop when you want it to," I told her. "You could end this right now with a word."

"Please, baby? Come on."

She strained at the bonds again, but she was still completely helpless, and I could've teased her 'til the sun came up and there wasn't a damned thing she could do about it but lie there and let me tantalize her. She was paddling her feet and clutching at her hand ties impatiently, and I figured she was just about at her limit now, so I stroked her hair.

"Ask me nicely," I told her.

"Please?" she pleaded. "Please fuck me now? If you don't, I swear to god, I think I'll die."

I smiled and reached for the first tie, waiting before I loosened it.

"What if we spent tomorrow night the same way, but with you doing me?" I asked.

"Sounds fun, but what if I didn't, just to pay you back for being such a tease?"

"Well, then, I guess I'd have to do this."

I brushed the pastry brush lightly over her cunt lips again, knowing what sweet torture it was.

"I'd have to say that's pretty nice," she lied.

"Yeah?" I asked, pushing the spoon handle into her about an inch or so. "What if I tell you you're really the one teasing me?"

She giggled.

"You'd only be half right."

I leaned down close to her ear, making her shiver as I kissed her temple.

"Well, what if I told you I'm never letting you go?"

I was no longer talking about her being tied up, and both of us knew it. She sighed and relaxed into the bed, a satisfied smile on her face.

"What would I say?" she asked me. "I'd say I'm pretty lucky."

PETTING ZOO

Rachel Kramer Bussel

W hen you truly love someone, you'll do anything for them—
and vice versa. That goes a long way toward explaining
what I was doing dressed in five-inch shiny leather boots, my
voluptuous body poured into a corset, wearing a long black wig
and holding a chain, which was attached to a collar, which was
attached to my husband, Mason. The collar was all he had on,
by my command. But my command was, ultimately, a response
to his request, one of many such pleas, during our increasingly
heated role-playing sessions. There he was, his thirty-two-year-
old, hairy, oversized body on full display not just to me but also
to a whole roomful of kinky people, mostly women. I smiled as
I stared down at my pet for the night. I'd gotten used to the role
I now proudly played, but getting there took some time, and a
whole lot of love.

We'd been married for just over a year before somehow, my
buff, seemingly butch hubby, who loved to race his motorcycle
when we ventured out of the city, who was proud of his home-

cooked steaks, who grew a beard and disdained the "pretty boys" who got proper haircuts rather than having their wives trim their tresses, revealed to me one day that what he wanted most was to worship at my feet; to be my servant, my slave, my pet. Inside his macho exterior lurked the heart of a pure submissive. He'd never done it, but he'd apparently spent the last six months thinking about submitting, thinking about giving it up to me, his wife who usually could be found on all fours taking his gigantic cock in my pussy and once in a while in my ass. Instead of my bending over, he wanted me to tower over him. Okay, there was a little more that he wanted—like the chance to lick anonymous women's pussies, to be used like a toy, but all that only worked if I was the one "making" him do it.

It was a revelation, the first time he said it. My mind whirred with this new side of him, more surprised that he'd kept the fantasy from me than that he possessed it in the first place. It's not like we were shy and retiring, or never talked about sex; we made sure to keep our sex life as lively as it had started out, after our whirlwind, very hot romance, which included joining the mile-high club, plenty of phone sex and all sorts of sharing of dirty talk. I'd thought that in the year and a half we'd been together we'd unearthed each other's every secret; not that I was bored or anything, but I felt like we'd grown into ourselves, our marriage, and were at a point where we could finish each other's sentences. But apparently, there were things I still had to learn. I was in the middle of spinning a tale of me punishing an imaginary wisp of a girl I'd bring home, telling her how she'd sucked his cock the wrong way, when something shifted.

"You're gonna punish her really hard, right? Spank her ass?" His voice betrayed his excitement. The truth is, we weren't really entertaining the idea of a threesome, but it was the fantasy, the image, the idea that we were both responding to. I wasn't opposed to adding another woman—or man—into the mix someday, but not just yet. First I wanted to see how far we could take our own filthy fantasies.

"Yeah, you want to see that, right?" As I was talking, he turned over, and there was his ass, right before me. I cupped his cheeks and before I knew it I was giving Mason a demonstration of just what I would do to our mystery girl.

"You want me to tie you up and have women come over and sit on your face, is that what you're telling me?" I asked him one night as I myself straddled his pretty face, giving him his fill of his favorite meal. By then, I'd gotten used to our favorite fantasy scenario, had started to think of myself the way Mason thought of me, at home and when I was outside of it. I'd never been with anyone, man or woman, who was so eager for oral—even me, and I can't get enough cock down my throat, when I'm with the right person. His enthusiasm in turn engendered my own, but what I loved most was feeling him tremble when I talked dirty to him, when I spun tales of all the wicked things I was discovering I'd like to do to him.

I'm not naturally the dominant type; I haven't always taken the pride I do now in seeing a man cowering before me, but Mason has turned me into the kind of woman who loves a cruel smile, a harsh look, who loves to fling her boot out and watch him scurry to pull it off. That attitude has carried over into my professional life, where I've risen up the ranks of the cosmetics company I started at as a secretary; now I'm a vice president.

I thought for a moment about my climb up the corporate ladder as I watched Mason crawl on the ground, surrounded by beautiful women. This was his dream come true, and watching his ass—his middle-aged, hairy ass; the one I thought of as mine to enjoy—made me smile. In a way, I was doing this for him, but in so many other ways, I was doing it for me. I stood taller when he got on his knees. I got wet when he groveled, and I got a thrill out of seeing the other women coo over him. He truly was like a pet, or a toy, and thinking of him that way only made me love him more. I also knew he'd never be the type to cheat; why would he, when I allow him to lick all the pussies he wants? Well, that's not entirely true.

When he crawled over to me and I leaned down so he could kiss his way up from my cleavage to my neck, and then he whispered in my ear, "Mistress?" I had a feeling I knew what was coming.

"Yes, pet?"

"There is a woman who I'd like to play with. She's over there and she has a beautiful flogger and…"

"And what?" I prompted, knowing it would be a struggle for him to praise her without somehow denigrating me. Watching his mouth open and close amused me—and aroused me. I was pleased to find that I wasn't just doing this for him, because that one-sided type of sacrifice can ruin any relationship, even a kinky one.

"And…she's looking for someone to torture."

"And you think you'd be just the right someone?" I asked him.

"Because I…" he paused. "Because I want to try something new. You know I'm devoted to you, Mistress, one hundred percent. I want everyone to watch and see how much I can take, and be jealous of you that you get to take home such an obedient boy." I smiled. It was a good answer, a way of spinning his own urgent desire into something that would give me some street cred, too. I wanted Mason to be happy, because without that, what was the point of our marriage? And by now I was curious to see what exactly would happen when I let him roam and play.

"Okay, you have my permission, but you better be done in

half an hour, or I'm going to drag you out of here by your hair and make you crawl around outside on the street wearing only what you're wearing now." Of course I'd never do such a thing, but it was plausible enough that he didn't need to know my true intentions. I could tell that my "threats" were part of what got him excited, and doing that for him in turn made me feel like a good wife, not in a traditional way, but in my way. Yes, call me crazy, but I saw my act of issuing bold threats of bodily harm almost, well, romantic.

Mason was overjoyed, and if he'd had a tail, it would've been wagging. Instead, his cock bobbed up and down. "But you know that your cock belongs to me, right? We don't have to get you a cage for it, do we?" I reached down and stroked his balding head, my gentle hand playing good cop to my words' bad cop.

"Of course not. I'd never let another woman touch me there." Mason sounded almost offended that I'd even mention it.

"Okay then, you head on over, I'll be by to watch soon. Be good for her; I don't want to hear any complaints." I unclipped the chain but kept the collar on him, smiling as I watched him go, then stood and surveyed my surroundings. I'd slowly turned into the kind of woman who belonged in such a setting, a woman who could walk proudly, even in five-inch heels, and not feel self-conscious about her breasts practically hanging out of a corset. It's taken me a while to become comfortable with my voluptuous body, to not want to whittle it down to a size six or four, but to be proud of its ten or twelve. Even with Mason's love and devotion, it wasn't until we started coming to parties like these that I truly saw what the extra weight could do for me, how it helped me to tower over men like Mason, how it made the snap of a whip sound that much louder, how my heft made me more of a woman, not less.

I owed that to him, though I'd never quite gotten around

to telling my husband that. He didn't need to know my every innermost thought; I'd learned that that was one of the keys to a happy marriage. I walked toward him and found him with a bright red butt plug sticking out of his ass, one that looked on the large side. I knew he'd never worn one before; we'd talked about it, but that was as far as it had gotten. His lips were wrapped around the heel of a shiny black boot, which was attached to a strikingly beautiful woman with long, glossy black hair, shiny pink lips and layers of mascara. She looked like she was in her early twenties, and for a moment, jealousy threatened to undo my inner goddess.

But then I walked closer and saw the look of joy on Mason's face as he sucked, his eyes closed. I stepped back when a loud cracking sound issued right near me; it was a whip, landing on Mason's ass. He let out a yelp, but went right back to sucking the boot. The woman looked up at me and winked, the perfect action to pacify my nerves. She seemed to know that the man sucking on her boot was mine, all mine, and that she was only borrowing him. He was her pet not for the night, but for the moment.

"Is this your owner, slave?" she called down to him, pointing toward me.

Mason's face flushed red before he said, "Yes, Ma'am, that's Mistress Stephanie." He'd called me "Ma'am" and even "Mistress," but never "Mistress Stephanie," like a proper title.

"Is my property behaving?" I asked, just as the woman with sleek white hair sent another crack of the whip against his butt.

"Oh yes, he is," the first woman said, running the tip of her shoe along his cheek. He smiled up at her while I surveyed the scene. Just then I spied a young man who looked like he could use a spanking. I knew this because he was holding a somewhat forlorn sign saying Spank Me. It's My Birthday.

If Mason could indulge, so could I. "I'll be back," I said, and knew Mason would be curious about where I'd gone. I didn't need to watch him at work to know how grateful he would be to me for granting him this excursion.

"What's your name and how old are you?" I kept my voice husky and severe.

"George. I'm twenty-one."

"A baby, are you? Well, George, that's my husband right over there," I said, pointing toward Mason. George gasped, then looked back at me. "Maybe someday you'll be lucky enough to be married to a woman like me, but right now, I have a little time on my hands and I wouldn't want to see a birthday boy like you not get the spanking you deserve. I'm going to give you one smack for each year you've been alive, and you're going to thank me for them, loudly. You're going to say, 'Thank you, Mistress Stephanie.' Do you understand me?"

"Yes, Mistress Stephanie," he said, and proceeded to position himself across my lap. I pulled down his pants and gave him a nice, firm slap. The sound echoed in the air and I soon became enamored of the way this lithe young man reacted to each smack. I didn't forget about Mason, exactly, but he wasn't foremost in my mind. I knew he was in good hands—or feet, as it were.

"Louder!" I roared as I reached the eighth blow, wanting to make sure Mason heard, wanting him to know that while I was here mostly at his behest, this wasn't all about him. Pets don't control their owners. By twelve, George's ass was very red, and very warm. My palm was stinging, so I took more time between slaps, using that time to tease his asshole with my index finger, to pinch his enflamed cheeks, to dig my nails into his back. Spanking him was giving me all sorts of ideas of what I wanted to do with Mason.

I pictured myself punishing Mason—it didn't matter for what—and that added extra vigor to my smacks. The last few were extra loud and extra hard, and when I let George stand up and kiss my hand, he was breathing heavily. I walked back over to check on Mason. He had a hand mark across his cheek, and was sitting with his legs tucked beneath him, waiting for me.

"Did he behave?" I asked the Mistress whose name I hadn't caught.

"Well enough," she said.

"And?" I prompted Mason.

"Thank you very much," he said to each of the women he'd had the pleasure of bottoming to.

"Now it's time to go home. And you're going to wear just your rubber shorts." At his look, I smiled. "Yes, of course I brought them for you; I wouldn't let you walk around with your cock, the one that belongs to me, hanging out. You can also wear your shoes." I could tell he wanted to protest, that he thought maybe I was taking our D/s arrangement a little too far, but I'd granted him his wish, and he was going to grant me mine. That was how things worked in this brave new kinky world.

"Yes, Mistress Stephanie," he said. I grabbed his cock and led him toward our bags, squeezing just a little harder than I needed to. And I liked the way it felt. Our night was far from done, but we'd each gotten something that we'd wanted. I may not be naturally dominant, but I'm a fast learner. And I have the best teacher a Mistress could ask for.

NORMAL

Charlotte Stein

I guess we look like any normal couple. More normal than any normal couple, in fact. He wears plaid shirts and khakis, and I wear twinsets, and we go to town meetings. While at the town meetings, we eat the normal amount of free cookies and sandwiches and sometimes we have punch. Everybody shakes our hands and no one averts his gaze, so I know we at least seem ordinary.

But I know they'd think something different if they were with me in the entryway to our little normal house with its painted shutters and the welcome mat at the door. Normal couples don't do what we're doing, with the autumn air still rushing in from outside and his hand just reaching to put the keys on their hook.

That's right. We have a key hook and winter jackets and a doorbell that chimes the theme from "The Simpsons." We also have a game where I put two fingers to the back of his neck and say, "If you move a muscle, I'll blow your fucking head off."

He doesn't move a muscle. We've played this game often

enough for him to know not to. His hand hovers near the hook, as still as if some gunman had really come up behind him and pressed the barrel to his skin, but more impressive than that is his other arm, the one that's slightly curled because he was also going to take off his jacket and now he's caught. It must be uncomfortable, being frozen in that half-caught-in-a-sleeve position, but he manages it. He always manages it.

One time I snuck up on him as he was bending over to run a bath, and he stayed like that, too. Hunched, barely balanced on anything stable, one hand reaching, just like now. And he'd remained that way for as long as I required him to—though when you think about it, what sort of person would refuse to with a gun pushed into the small of his back?

It's these little things that make me certain he believes the act, utterly. He believes it in a weird way, as though some part of his brain is always just waiting for this and inside that part, he's sure: *I would freeze in position until my muscles burned and my head swam, if this really happened.*

Though the word *this* has a little leeway in it, because I know what he does if he's actually threatened. One time some guy tried to grab my purse and he yanked him back by his jacket and punched him in the face. Really quick, too, as though he didn't have to think about it and the guy should just get punched. He's a big man, so it's not as though he has anything to be afraid of.

But he's afraid of this, because this isn't some guy mugging us in a parking lot. *This* is something else altogether, something weird that started for reasons undisclosed. I want to say it started because we were messing around with water pistols and somehow I pinned him down, though that word somehow has a lot of leeway in it, too. It bends as far as *he kind of let me* and *I kind of liked it,* and then I said, "I'll smack you with the butt of this thing if you don't stop your fucking squirming," and he looked...I don't know. The way he sometimes looks when I go down on him.

It's very easy to tell, on him. It's how we ended up going out in the first place. I was shy and he was too cute, and I didn't realize he wanted me until I gave him a friendly hug and saw his flushed face afterward. I rarely know when a man is progressing toward turned on, but it had been pretty obvious, then. He gets all hot eyed and fidgety, and the things he says aren't as smooth as the things he was saying before.

He can be smooth when he wants to be. Charming, even. Lots of girls liked him, before I got him. But lots of girls probably wouldn't understand him saying—smoothly, of course— "Would it be such a bad idea if we played that game again? You know. The one with the water pistols."

Though of course we don't need water pistols, now. My fingers are enough, like little kids playing cops and robbers, only he's the cop and I'm the robber and I always somehow get one up on him. Even when it's just my fingers. Even though he's a foot taller than me and built so big it sometimes makes me shiver just looking at him.

I'm wet already, and I don't know if it's because of him and the way he smells tonight—like that good aftershave he bought—or because of the game. The game. The one that's probably taking over our lives.

I mean, we play it at least once a month, now. That's bad, right? Or is it just bad that we play it at all? Normal couples play games, I know it. But they don't sound like our games—or maybe they do.

Just the other way around.

"Please don't hurt me," he says, and I wonder who he imagines I am. Is that what this fantasy's about? Him imagining me as someone else, someone rougher—maybe even a man?

Just because he reacted differently when it really was a man—that doesn't mean anything. That was reality. This is fantasy. It's different, when you can control all the parameters. It's different when you know someone might really hurt you or hurt your wife.

It could be that he secretly wishes I was big and strong and masculine.

Though when I really think about it...the things he's actually asked for...the ones he's dared to voice despite the fact that neither of us really discuss this...they were all very one way. You don't ask someone to push her breasts into your back when you want to pretend it's a man attacking you. And somehow I doubt you'd need someone's pussy all over your face, if you were desperately craving dick.

But even so these little doubts linger in my mind, until I'm not really sure what I'm thinking anymore. I just do it, instead, and that's much better. I tell him to move forward into our house and not to make any sudden moves, and he obeys me exactly in these little, tentative, shuffling steps.

Just like the real thing. Though I'm not sure how I know what the real thing is like. Or why I enjoy this, if I let myself think of things like that—how scared and full of hesitation someone would be, with a real gun to the back of his head. How his mind would race with everything some pervert could do.

Only I'm the pervert. Once we're safe inside, I tell him to start taking off his clothes, and there's really nothing more you can say about that. It's weird and wrong and my body hums with it until I think I might pass out. My clit is a swollen heartbeat between my legs and my nipples are diamond hard, and when I hear the jangle of his belt and the rasp of his zipper, everything gets worse. Or better, depending on your point of view.

I wonder if it's the wrongness that makes it sweeter. That

vague idea that this is *his* weird fantasy, but *I'm* the one getting some illicit, bizarre sort of pleasure out of it. Does he know I do? I can't see how he could fail to. Whenever we get to the good part I'm always as wet as rain, and I come hard. I come with barely a hand or a mouth on me—I can just slide down his cock and that's it, right there.

I suppose it's the power dynamic. The shift. Something like that. But when he's stripped from the waist down and I can see the strong shape of his good thighs and the almost-tender curve of his ass, I'm not so certain anymore.

I want to bite that ass. I want to scratch it. I want to leave perfect red streaks all over his pale, unblemished skin, so that he's just a mixture of white and red and black. And that seems even more wrong than the thrill I get, the pleasure of putting two fingers to the back of his neck. I mean, I love my husband. I love him truly, madly, deeply. There's no urge in me to hurt him, not really. We've never so much as exchanged brutal words, the way some couples do. Just the thought of seeing his face fall as I say something rotten makes me curdle inside.

The rotten things don't ever even occur to me, because he's a wonderful man. He doesn't leave his socks out; he's never late. He supports me in everything I do and it feels like something natural to lean into him when I'm in need or feeling blue.

And yet here we are.

"Is that enough?" he asks, but he already knows the answer. No, the pants are not enough.

"All off, bitch," I say, and though the word feels kind of silly in my mouth he shivers on hearing it. Shivers, and obeys. I step back and he pulls his shirt over his head, then the T-shirt underneath.

It feels kind of weird to keep the pretense of a gun up, clasping one hand over the other and poking one little finger out, but I do it anyway. Because that's as much a part of the game as his acquiescence. The feel of that fakery against my palm makes me strong and like a different person, until I can feel my shaking legs growing stiff and firm and my aching body aches harder, hotter.

"What are you going to do to me?" he asks, which only makes me think of the things I've done before. All of them make my face heat. Once, I made him masturbate while I took pictures— I have no idea why. These things just come to me like the next bead on a rosary I'm fumbling through, and I never quite know what it's going to look like until it's there in front of me.

"I haven't decided yet," I say, and he moans. It excites me, that moan—because I recognize it so intimately. It's the same one he lets out when I'm pushing up against him or maybe rubbing him through his pants, and he knows, he just knows that soon we'll be making love.

But then he says, "Please don't hurt me," as a little chaser to the too-excited sound, and then I'm all mixed up and inside out again. A little kick of heat goes through me and I tell him to shut his fucking mouth. I tell him I'll hurt him if I want to, and nothing he does will stop me.

He's panting now. Harsh and rattling, like he's trying to get it under control.

"You feel so safe in your neat little world, don't you," I say. I'm not asking.

"I..." he starts, but doesn't finish.

"Until right now, I bet," I tell him, then press my two fingers to the naked small of his back. When that doesn't provoke a strong enough response, I run them down his spine, over and over. I wait, until he tries to squirm away from me.

And then I get a fistful of his hair and yank his head back.

He makes a little sound low down in his throat, which lets me know the move has shocked him. And my teeth suddenly in

the soft flesh close to his shoulder, the tauter flesh over the round
bone—that shocks him, too.

But I can tell he likes it at the same time. I know for a fact
that he loves having his hair pulled and he always goes limp
when I bite him, though it's neither of those things that confirms
how arousing he finds it. It's the shock and his reaction to it. His
sudden wateriness, like his knees have turned to jelly.

He likes it best when I'm unexpected. As though this could be
real, it could all be real, and there are no limits to my brutality.

I think it's this idea that pushes me farther. Like he's goading
me into more, and I give it. I grasp his fat, stiff cock just as he's
getting his bearings from the bite and the hair pull, and I squeeze
hard.

Though it isn't the feel of me that makes him moan and gasp,
I know. It's what I say; it's the words that force their way out of
me—they're the ones to blame.

"Oh, I see," I tell him, and I barely have to say anything more.
My tone is so cruel, so cruel—god, I never imagined I could be
capable of this much cruelty. I sound like the curving, sharp edge
of something nastily mocking, and his moan melts down into
embarrassment. Mortification, in fact.

"One of *those*, huh?" I ask, and he tries to curl away from the
press of my palm. The squeeze and release I get up to, with my
teasing, torturing hand. It always amazes me, at this point, how
I manage to manipulate a body so much bigger than mine—how
I can twist him back against me and get my hand around him
and whisper in his ear. Though secretly I suppose I know he's
helping me. I can feel him putting his weight on the balls of his
feet. Holding himself, for me.

Is it weird, if that turns me on more than any pretense at
reality?

"No, I'm not, I'm not," he says, which only makes me wonder

what he thinks I mean. What *those* am I talking about? What kind of weirdo does he think my mind is conjuring up?

"Your body doesn't lie," I say, and I feel so sick, so wrong, I'm such a bad person.

Until he moans and pushes into my hand, and then I don't know what I am.

"Get down on there, you little slut," I say, then watch as he does. He even does it in just the way I'd imagined—crouched on his knees on the couch, elbows on the arm so he's kind of on all fours.

Though I don't know why I imagined that. I've gone past the fumbling and into some kind of insane autopilot, and it's like someone else is telling him to reach into the drawer next to him and get out the baby oil that I don't want to think about why we keep there.

We keep it there in case our elbows get dry, right? A dry elbow emergency in the middle of watching "The Wire." Right?

Somehow, I don't think dry elbows make a person breathe as hard as he's doing. Or shake as much as he's doing. And from here I can see the slant of his gorgeous face, and it's flushed and weird and any second he's probably going to come all over the couch.

I think I want him to. No, I definitely want him to.

"Now make yourself nice and wet for me," I say, though my insides balk at the words and I'm halfway certain he won't understand what I mean. It's too filthy. He'll never get it.

But then he says "Okay, okay, just don't hurt me," far too quickly. And he doesn't beg, even though most of the time he at least puts up a little resistance. This time, he slicks up his fingers—just two of them, as though he's done it many, many times before—and slides them between the cheeks of his perfect ass.

As though he's done that before, too.

Though he struggles, when it comes to the thing I didn't even know I wanted. Or he wanted. And I can see he's never really done this before, at least—penetrated himself with two fumbling fingers. His body's long and it's a hard reach, and when he turns a little I can see the mixture of emotions on his face. How they've fought until they've made his expression slack. He can't hold them all together.

He doesn't know what he's doing, and it's then I know. I have to help him.

"Move," I tell him, as though he's just a nuisance. He's in the way and I'm going to show him how it's done, even though I've got no idea.

Lucky, really, that it's so easy. I just kneel behind him and stroke between the cheeks of his ass until he stops jerking or trying to jolt away from me, and then real sudden he spreads open beneath just ever so slight a pressure, and I'm sinking one finger all the way in.

Of course, it's gentler than a real attacker would be. But he still begs and says "No no no," and tightens around that intruding thing, to the point where I'm sure I should stop. He doesn't like it. This isn't what he wants. It's hot and amazing and the weirdest thing I've ever done, but he doesn't want it.

So I go to pull away. I think of some bullshit thing I can say that will keep us in the game but let him off the hook, like, *Knew you couldn't take it*—but that's the moment he chooses to push back against my hand. The way I do, when he's got me on all fours and he's just teasing me with his cock, just promising to thrust in hard and fast until I'm sobbing.

I think he sobs, too.

"You like that, huh? Look at you, taking it. Whore," I say, because I'm bad but he's worse. He tells me "Ohhhhh, yes I am,

I am, I'm such a whore," and pushes and pushes back against the finger I'm fucking him with as though he can hardly contain himself.

I can't concentrate on how it feels—silky, I'll probably think later, and vise tight—or whether it means he really does want a man to fuck him. Maybe, though I don't think wanting to experience something in your ass is quite the same as wanting some hairy big-thighed fucker doing you—but I can concentrate on how it feels for *me*. I'm too hot inside my clothes and I've soaked through my panties, while the urge to rub myself against the curve of his ass grows immense, impossible.

I need to come. I think he needs to, too. He's babbling things that are not words and every now and then I catch him trying to push his swollen cock against the silk of the couch. I tell him I'm going to fuck him, now, and he tries harder, moans louder, his eyes barely seeing me when I force him to turn over.

I slide my finger from his ass and he rocks back and forth as though feeling the absence too strongly, but when I push my little fake gun into the soft place just below his jaw, he goes still—the kind of still that suggests a trembling tension, just below the surface.

"Don't you fucking move while I do this," I say, but he's too far gone to stop himself making noise. Or jerking upward as I wriggle out of my panties and get myself over him.

"Please," he says, though I can't tell if he means *please do* or *please don't*. He just stares up at me with his dark, too intense eyes and waits for me to slide my embarrassingly slick pussy down over his tensely hard cock.

It feels like bursting. He feels much too big, and I'm much too worked up, and I can hardly do the thing I usually do—fuck him hard and fast and brutal, as though I'm sticking something in him rather than taking something in.

So to compensate, I get a fistful of his hair. I clench it tight between my fingers and call him a slut, a dirty slut who just loves getting fucked by anyone, anyhow. I think of lurid porn movies and a million men saying *You want every hole filled, don't you, whore?* and it comes easier, then. I tell him he wants something in his ass and something in his mouth and something around his cock, and though I'm sure it should sound silly, it doesn't, somehow.

It sounds dirty and hot and nasty as fuck, and even more so when he pants "Yeah, yeah, I want to be used, I want to be used up."

I think it's that word—*used*. I think about how many times I've felt that way in my life, just because someone did something he could never bear to. And then I come hard, in great breaking swells, with his cock still jerking inside me and my hand still in his hair and not a thing touching my clit.

He can do that. And it makes it better when he follows almost immediately after, hands suddenly on my thighs as his hips snap upward, uncontrollably. I can feel him coming thick and strong, and it's good enough that he can't seem to make any sound. His mouth just makes one big O and his eyes go back, and I know, I know, I understand.

What he needs—it's not the same as what's normal or good or right. It's something different and strong, and it guides like a hand on the back. Like a gun at the nape of his neck. And that's okay, because it guides me, too. I'm bleak and blank with it.

And even if they could see how normal we're not, I'd do it anyway. I would, I swear I would. The gun is at the nape of my neck, and I can't do anything but.

EVERYTHING SHE'D ALWAYS WANTED

Ariel Graham

The plane began its descent exactly on time. Gwendolyn watched as Seattle grew closer, as the plane cleared a million trees and bodies of water and dropped down with a thud that should have been reassuring.

David leaned in close as she stared out the window at the airport rushing by. His breath on her neck was warm. She knew he was savoring every minute, knew what he was going to do and say before he did it.

"Nervous?"

His breath warmed the silver Eternity Collar around her throat and Gwen put a hand up to touch it. She still wasn't used to the thing: its weight, the way it turned hot and cold in response to the temperature around her.

What it meant.

No, she wanted to say in response. Not nervous. She could deny him that pleasure and tell him she wasn't nervous and it wouldn't even be outside their agreement, really, the part of the agreement where she was supposed to tell him the truth about everything. She wasn't nervous.

She was terrified.

She turned from the window where men in orange vests were waving the plane in despite the fact that they stood slightly behind it and, without a rearview mirror, the pilot couldn't possibly see them. Maybe they were waving the baggage carts in. Around Gwen and David, people were standing, beginning to clatter items from overhead bins. This was usually the time Gwen found it hardest not to shove and push her way off the plane, wishing she could explain to those left tumbled in her wake that if they would only pay attention to all the obvious signs—tray tables in upright positions, flight attendants strapped in, ground coming up to meet them—they all could have been ready to go, like she was. They'd have been out of the way.

Today she was in no hurry. Fear clawed its way around inside her chest. Her overhead luggage held her camera and laptop, a silken blindfold, a set of shackles. Her checked luggage held more.

The skirt and heels she wore, so different from her usual travel-wear of jeans and high-tops, kept reminding her she was here. The skirt brushed loosely around her calves. The shoes pinched her feet. Things were different now.

Her heartbeat skidded about, too fast, too hard.

A second pulse beat between her legs.

The rental car was housed deep in the parking garage, away from the entrance and the rental agency booths. David caught her before she headed to the passenger door. She turned to look at him, his dark hair rumpled, his pale blue eyes avid. She stood still as he finished loading their suitcases into the trunk then walked her to the car door. She didn't climb in when he opened it, but waited for his command.

"Climb onto the seat on your hands and knees," he said.

She swallowed and tried not to look for whatever security cameras or guards might be nearby. The rental car smelled like air freshener and someone's leftover cologne, impersonal and public. She kept her head up, kneeling on the seat, and felt him move in close behind her, blocking her from the view of any casual passersby. His hands came down on her hips, and he held her for the space of several heartbeats before he moved, lifting her loose skirt, flipping it up over her back. He grunted in approval at her stockings and put a hand between her legs, his fingers covering her mons, his palm cupping her.

"You're so wet," he said.

She shivered and prayed he wouldn't request anything else of her. Not here. Not now. This wasn't what she was ready for. She'd had no time to imagine it, to work through it in her mind.

Which was why he wanted it. She felt his hands hook under the elastic of her thong, pulling it slowly over her hips, down her thighs and letting it pool around her knees. The cool northwest air stroked her wet flesh. Gwen groaned, desperate and ashamed.

David must've stepped back then, because she felt the air all around her, and she almost broke from the position he'd put her in. She sensed David's pause, knew he was watching her to see what she'd do. Whether she'd panic or whether she'd obey.

Everything she'd always wanted, he'd said, enough times she thought she believed him, but the fear—she hadn't counted on the fear.

That she'd be seen. Possibly? That she wouldn't be seen.

David's belt buckle clanked, a familiar sound, followed by the somehow savage and sensual sound of his belt being pulled free of its loops.

This time she did groan, just a little, in the instant before David's belt smacked down against her upturned ass.

He kept it short, just six strokes across her cheeks. Anything else would've been awkward. Getting arrested wasn't part of the weekend plan. Before he told her she could pull herself together, he slid two fingers deep inside her.

"You are so fucking wet," he said, and then, "Move your knees. One at a time. Up." And her thong flowed away from her, tossed into the foot well of the passenger side.

"Good girl," David said, and she stirred, trying to remember what she'd been afraid of and why she should move. She said his name, very thickly, and he laughed. "Oh, no, not yet, my pet. Not for quite a while."

They went shopping in the afternoon, to bookstores and fetish shops, to department stores and adult stores. Gwen, her pulse kicking higher, wrapped her hands around her forearms across her lower back, getting as close to her elbows as she could. In one leather shop the man behind the counter watched them as if they weren't somewhere people habitually went on leashes. In another, the clerk with the pink hair and double nose rings watched them as if afraid they were going to create some kind of spectacle. But David only wandered with Gwen, showing her the future to come with cuffs, ropes, blindfolds, floggers, cats, paddles, crops and whips. Heat climbed in Gwen's cheeks and she followed him to a dark corner where he showed her restraints, plugs and dildos and another where he backed her into a cage and at a short, sharp "Sir!" from the pink-haired clerk, didn't close it, but laughed at Gwen's expression.

"One day," he said, "I'll make you write out a list of punishments you'd truly like to not experience and then do them to you for the next ten days."

Gwen raised her eyes to his. "It's not D/D, Sir," she said. David nodded as if she'd just made his point. "Even slaves can misbehave."

The party wouldn't start until ten. David bought her pizza for dinner. When she raised her eyebrows at his choice, he grinned, looking somewhat like a demonic little boy. "It's not like you're going to eat much regular dinner. And you'll need your strength."

She shuddered, and ate pepperoni pizza and watched seagulls in the parking lot. David took her hand across the table and early evening sunlight gleamed off his wedding band. They'd been married nine years when he told her some of the things he'd been wanting and it was as if someone had lit a fuse under Gwen. David had talked for what seemed hours, explaining he wanted a Master/slave relationship, and what he would expect of her, and how much he loved her, and what he thought her desires really were.

He promised if she said no they wouldn't change from who they were, he'd put that side of himself away, somehow—and she'd interrupted him, kissing him hard, her mouth bruising his, her fingers tangling in his hair until he stopped her, and held her, without speaking, then rose and took her hand and led her upstairs to their bedroom, streetlight pouring in the windows, and they never bothered with the lights, never even bothered to fully undress. And still it was their last vanilla coupling.

He'd wakened her the next morning with a harsh spanking and followed that by shoving her down under the covers to give him a blow job. She'd adapted quickly, something in her recognizing what she'd been searching for. She started shaving, started dressing for him in heels and stockings and often nothing else. Exercise and diet took on new meaning. David took pride in his possessions. When he collared her, she panicked, and panicked again several times after that. David didn't bother to talk her down. He just waited her out. She was his. She couldn't do anything about the collar, so why bother panicking?

They talked about what they wanted, Gwen naked and kneeling in front of him on the floor, and even so she somehow hadn't thought that it would ever all come to pass, all those things she'd said on that long lazy summer afternoon between the blow jobs and the spankings and the times he'd play with her until she almost exploded and then make her sit still, on the floor, on the couch, hands behind her back.

Pain. Humiliation. Forced exhibitionism. Strangers touching her, commanding her, playing with her; everything but fucking her, he'd promised. That was his alone.

She hadn't really expected it would come to pass. Even when they ordered plane tickets, it had always been in the future. Something she didn't have to think of yet.

"Are you going to eat that?"

Gwen stared at the pizza, then at David, and shook her head.

"Come on, then."

In the hotel room he stripped her, leaving her only her shoes and stockings, then tied her facedown to the bed, arms and legs spread-eagled. "Lift a little to the right," he said, kneeling on the bed behind her, and when she did he wedged two of the hard foam pillows under the edge of her hip and thigh, then leaned over her other side and, once secured, her lower body rested far enough above the bed so that she couldn't grind or rub or touch.

David drew one finger lightly down the back of her neck, along her spine, gently, teasingly, lovingly. He traced the dimples above her ass, cupped her cheeks, drew them apart just slightly. He ran his finger over her lips, along her clit, touched just the outside edges of her asshole.

Gwen writhed. She thrashed. When she started to moan, he picked up her discarded thong and wadded it into her mouth. Then he went back to stroking. Gently. Faster and slower. Over her clit. Over and over her clit, and lips, and ass.

He let her up three hours before the party, told her to go shower and get completely ready. Gwen, flushed, desperate for release, nodded but took in the time.

"We have time yet," she said.

David nodded, seemingly not annoyed she hadn't just followed his orders. "Yes. I want to give you plenty of time to anticipate."

She dressed to his specifications, taking her time because he'd given her so much of it. Every minute that ticked by made her more nervous. Every article of clothing made her hotter.

The shoes were red, long and pointed with four-inch heels, because anything more made her fall flat on her face. Thin straps surrounded her ankles. Her stockings ended about the place her skirt came down to. The skirt itself was nothing special, just short and black, but her top was as tight and red as her shoes, a cinched corset top. She thought she looked like an erotic, adult version of Heidi. All she needed were braids instead of the sleek, pulled-back style her auburn hair was restrained in. But clothes didn't matter that much. The skirt would come off at some point during the party, leaving her with flame-red tap pants to match the corset top, and David promised somebody at some point was bound to remove even those.

The party was being held in an old Victorian, three stories and a basement tucked discreetly into a gentrifying neighborhood whose other residents doubtless had no idea what was going on inside.

She made it to the front stairs before she balked. At the last minute it seemed that all that mattered was explaining away the cost of everything they'd done to get here, why it was a good thing anyway, why she was perfectly happy and satisfied, and why they could just *go*. Right *now*.

David waited her out, pulling her into a thicket of roses off the front walk so they didn't hinder the arrival of other guests. A few people said hello, but night had fallen, a true October night with wood smoke scenting the salty Pacific Northwest air. David just listened and breathed, and for Gwen the terror jacked higher, that he was listening. That might mean that he would take her away. That he might not. She wanted it. So much. Had dreamed about it: the voyeurism, the exhibitionism. The strangers. The pain. She didn't know what she wanted most. She wanted it all. The trip, the shopping, the anticipation, the inevitable release at David's hands; the fantasies, anyway—they weren't enough.

She wanted it.

She craved it. As much as she ever had. She swallowed the terror and slowly made herself stop talking.

He smiled at her then, and took her hand, and led her inside.

Just inside the door a woman stood lashed to the staircase balustrade. Gwen did a double take, after promising herself she wouldn't, not even once, and then smiled, to show she wasn't at all shocked or surprised at the naked woman or the ropes that bound her tightly, her breasts jutting out between the ropes. She had a feeling her smile would have fallen flat if only the girl had been even slightly aware of her. But the eyes Gwen looked into were dreamy, ecstatic and miles away.

"Let's go this way," David said, guiding her by the elbow, and Gwen let herself be led.

In the sitting room, a handful of people surrounded a banked fire. Some held glasses of cider. Some held each other. A few took part in slow, languid conversations. A redheaded pixie smiled brightly at David and Gwen and everyone arranged themselves a little to give them room.

"We're talking about the election and some of the scary conservatives running," she said, sliding across the couch so Gwen could sit beside her. The man on her other side said, "Scared conservatives works just as well," and someone laughed.

"I'm Angel," the redhead said. "It's my party. Are you the couple from Nevada?" She directed her question at David, who either looked less freaked out or less lustful or more aware than Gwen, she thought, and then, slowly, Gwen reached up and touched the Eternity Collar around her own throat. The cold metal was at once both tremendously reassuring and a bit of a shock. Mostly she realized that here it meant something. Something more than what it meant at home, with David, who loved her. Something more than it meant at work, where she hung charms off it or wove scarves through it.

Gwen took a look around the room at the couples, making mental guesses at relationships, and slid, quietly, to the floor at David's feet.

Her blood pumped hard and strong. Her breath came quick and shallow. Her sex felt wet and hot and swollen and she wanted more than anything for David to take over.

"Well, you didn't come all the way from Nevada to listen to the lot of us discuss politics," Angel said, standing. Tiny and fiery, Gwen thought she might be as tall as Angel was standing while Gwen was still sitting on the floor. "If you like, I'll give you a tour."

The three-story Victorian was full of shadows and vibrant or ominous or stark or moody lighting. Groups passed by wrapped around each other or trailing on leashes or following orders on definite missions. David walked beside Gwen and held her hand. No one blinked. Her collar stated her place. Her Master's choice was up to him, and David liked to touch her.

The kitchen was full of famished people in various stages of dress and undress. Marble countertops glittered with candle stubs and featured cold cuts and antipasto, pizza and cake and, forlorn, an entire ham no one apparently had the energy to deal with.

If it hadn't been for the absence of alcohol and the prevalence of cider, it would have looked like any party.

"C'mon," Angel said, and disappeared through a door Gwen had taken for a pantry.

Stone steps descended, worn and crumbling, leading down into a dank basement. The temperature changed instantly; a cold, clammy indication that everything had just changed.

They both stopped at the bottom of the stairs, David as frozen as Gwen.

The basement was a marvel.

Separated into sections, decorated and lighted to reflect the various activities, it sported six different kinky camps.

Gwen's throat closed instantly. David's grip on her hand tightened.

"Oh," Angel said, stiffening. "There's someone I need to talk to. Listen, just make yourselves at home. If you want to use equipment that's not in use, feel free. If you need something for a scene, look for someone with a green ribbon on their shirt. As long as you don't interrupt anything, you can pretty much observe anything you want."

Before either could answer, she gave them a fey girl grin and flickered away into a knot of people in the center of the basement.

"It's a little like a really weird craft show," Gwen said as they started around the perimeter of the room. They stopped at the edge of a group watching two women on spanking horses and the Dom in between working up a sweat with a flogger and a leather strap, alternating between implements and bottoms. One girl's face was red and wet, her fingers white-knuckling the horse. The other wore the distant dreamy gaze of the girl at the stairs. Every few strokes the man between them would stop and murmur questions at them and wait for answers.

David pressed himself tight behind her. "Looks like they're almost finished. Do you..."

She swallowed, afraid he'd hear it and longing to press her clit against the hard wood of the horse while David stood behind her, or maybe the man in the black T-shirt, wielding a crop or the strap, or even a wooden paddle. She wanted to feel wood against her naked bottom.

The fear crashed up inside her.

"Let's see more first."

His fingers tightened around hers and he followed her as they moved counterclockwise through the room, past rope play and suspension, the girl's breasts protruding and the man with her just clamping her nipples. Past a scene between three people neither of them could quite make out, but which seemed to be moving along just fine without them. Directly across from the stairs they came to a St. Andrew's cross, where a muscular man hung from silken bonds, his back red with marks but skin unbroken. His eyes were half closed and sweat beaded the dark beard stubble on his jaw. He looked ecstatic.

David crossed his arms over her breasts from behind. "Let me tie you up and spank you." Watching the man on the cross, Gwen licked her lips. But David was asking. She pressed the longing down.

"I want to see," she said. She did. But still. Two more stations, one with edgy knife play that made both of them tighten around each other and move on with more haste than they meant to exhibit. The last featured play piercing.

Her heart hammered. There was nothing more to see in the basement.

"So what's your pleasure?" he asked, his voice hot in her ear. His teeth nipped the outer curl where her piercings were.

I want, I want, I want, Gwen thought, but started to say, "Then what's upstairs?"

She got only to the word *up* before he slipped his fingers into her collar and used it to sink her slowly to her knees.

One or two people blinked at them, but they stood back out of the way of any play. David bent from the waist, his fingers still inside her collar, and whispered directly in her ear.

"When I release you, you are going to stand up and take off your skirt, fold it and place it over there." He indicated a table along one wall, all but lost in the blur Gwen's vision had become.

She nodded, swallowed, blinked, and nothing cleared. Her vision remained blurred. Her ears rang. Everything sounded loud and confusing, overwhelming.

The only thing you have to listen to is David.

At once she was able to take a full breath, and when David released her an instant later, she rose with some grace, took his proffered arm for support, and stepped out of her skirt. A couple more people paused to watch her, but in tap pants and what now felt like a very girlish corset top, she was more dressed than many of the other guests.

When she walked back to him, she saw the cross was now empty.

David smiled and held out his hand to her.

Something changed in that instant for her. Suddenly the fear tumbled away, the anticipation became joy. What had started as longing or craving or need was again.

He led her to the cross, arranged her to stand facing it. "I love you," he said, and fastened her left wrist to the wood. She stood still, as if her body no longer belonged to her, and waited for him to cross behind her and lift her right arm, securing that wrist.

"Make me proud."

She breathed in slowly through her mouth.

David fastened her ankles with shackles, right, then left. She faced the cross and wondered how many people had stopped to watch. It didn't matter, somehow. There was sensation. Anticipation. Fear fluttered around the edges. Her belly felt tight. Her sex felt drenched. David stood beside her, attaching a short lead from the cross to her collar.

"I don't want you to make a sound. Do you understand?"

She kept her eyes lowered. "Yes, Sir."

"Can you do that for me?"

Could she? She wanted to say she'd try. She wanted to ask if this had changed from what she wanted to what he wanted. She wanted to resist, to struggle or run or bolt, or balk again.

"Yes, Sir," Gwen said.

When the first lash fell, she felt almost as if she had already moved outside herself. She could hear David's steady breathing, and the sound of what she guessed was a crop whistling up through the air and then down at her. Gwen jolted at the blow, no harder or softer than those David had given her at home where she'd knelt on pillows or bent over chairs to receive whatever he wanted to give her.

This, here, with others, with acceptance, with ritual, was new. Different. The first blow bit like fire and the glow traveled instantly to her sex. She could have stopped then, dragged herself from the cross, dragged David from the party, made use of the rental car and every square inch of the hotel room.

The second snap burned. She let her head fall back. Her mind soared. Every image from the evening screamed in at her.

Third strike. He wanted her to stay quiet. She wanted to scream with joy.

Gwen bit her lip and stopped thinking, stopped counting, stopped analyzing. She gloried in sensation, in the warmth of pain spreading into want. At the idea of everyone around her. At being the center of attention in a group that probably held its breath for her, the way she had for the girls on the horses and the woman at the stairs. She wanted it all, she wanted everything, and as the crop snapped down faster, heating her ass, she knew if David let her down now she might just fall at his feet, too overwhelmed to do anything else.

She opened her eyes, wrapped her fingers around the chains that secured the cuffs and smiled up at the ceiling without seeing it.

David's hands brought her back. He unfastened the cuffs from the cross and led her to a dark quiet spot in the basement. Gwen leaned against him and felt foolish and somehow chilled. When she looked up at him, keeping her eyes downcast but tilting her face up, David took her chin in his hands and kissed her for a very long time. When he left off he took off his jacket and wrapped it around her. She had no idea where her skirt had gone or whether or not she was cold. Without thinking, she reached out for David's hand, instituting contact, and he didn't object. He took her hand in one of his and kissed her knuckles. In the other hand he held the camera. She remembered hearing photography wasn't allowed at play parties. She also remembered the flash going off.

David led her to the kitchen. The light dazzled Gwen. Light seemed to leap off the stone countertops, too bright, maybe like the light in an operating theater. Everyday objects—canisters, teakettles, a few people wearing jeans—seemed unfamiliar and out of place.

"Stay here," David said and placed her in a chair at a wide round kitchen table.

Gwen reached for him, suddenly alarmed, but he moved out of reach without noticing.

"I'm Lisa," said the girl across the table. "This is Cathy. And you?"

And me what? Gwen wondered, and looked from one to the other. Metal collars on the girls' throats sparkled with light and she realized they were slaves and that, for whatever reason, here in the kitchen it really was just sort of a normal party.

"Gwen," Gwen said.

"You look like you're having a really nice time," the first girl said and Gwen said something in return and the conversation turned to collars and somehow Gwen got lost in it and a little bit of time passed. Then David was back with a disposable cup of hot chocolate he pressed into her hands.

"Ladies, if you'll excuse us."

They found Angel and there was a flurry of conversation before Angel asked David something and then gave Gwen an unexpected hug and said she hoped to see her again, and shook David's hand and said no, it wasn't normally policy but she'd seen the shots and it was okay. Gwen stood, bemused, not really listening. Her attention was riveted on the hot chocolate.

Then they were outside where reality wasn't any more real because the fog had come in, shrouding streetlights and buffering reality away from them.

David laughed suddenly and Gwen pulled herself from her

long introspective stare at a halo surrounding a streetlight and said, slowly, "What?"

"Let's get you back to the hotel and get you some sleep."

She sharpened, then, a little more aware of the world and a lot more aware of herself. "Let's get back to the hotel," she agreed. "But sleep is the last thing I want to do."

This time when David tied her to the bed he didn't keep her hips suspended. He threw her down over the pillows so she could grind and probably only tied her up because the restraints were still on the bed.

"I don't think this is going to take long," he said, and thrust inside her.

Gwen felt her head roll up in pleasure as David slammed into her. She ground her sex into the pillows and felt his hands come down, slapping her ass, nothing like earlier. Everything like earlier. She felt him stiffen and go still in the instant before he shot into her, making a sound that tore from his throat. He shuddered and Gwen tightened around him as waves of orgasm began to roll over her and David leaned over her, gave her collar one tug, and said, "You're mine."

Gwen buried her face in the bedcovers and came, screaming.

She woke slowly the next morning. Hotel rooms always confused her, blackout curtains giving lie to the day outside. David was already awake and when he saw her open her eyes, he smiled and drew her to him, his arms cradling her close. "There are parties everywhere," he said. "I'm sure—"

She stiffened and pulled away from him. Just that fast the early morning lust seemed replaced with fear again. She'd wanted it. She'd done it. Surely now as fantasy material she could—

He startled her by laughing. "Backtracking, are you?"

She stumbled over her words as all the panic and planning and fear that had built up, like stage fright, flooded back in. Her stomach twisted. Once, yes, she'd managed it one time. That was enough.

"David, I loved it. It's just, I'm sure it's just a game to you and I can be happy—"

But he'd made a sort of conciliatory sound and pulled away from her, crossing the room to fetch the laptop and bring it back to the bed.

"David?"

He held up one finger, scrolled a bit, and turned it so she could see the screen.

Gwen's own face filled the screen, her eyes half open and as distant, dreamy and dazed as anyone's she'd seen at the party. She couldn't remember when the shot was taken but she knew, as he clicked through, she'd been attached to the cross, David using the crop on her and someone else taking pictures he'd had to get permission to take in the first place. When he got to the end of them, she eased the computer off his lap and started going through them again, seeing a Gwen she didn't remember being, remembering something she hadn't quite understood the first time around. She felt warm, glowing, safe and content. She nodded, and knew he understood why she nodded, and she didn't look away from the screen. Her face, flushed. Ecstatic. Full of lust.

Gwen smiled and made plans for the future.

ABOUT THE
AUTHORS

JANINE ASHBLESS has had two collections of erotic fairy, fantasy and paranormal stories and three paranormal erotic novels published by Black Lace. Her short stories have appeared in numerous anthologies including *Best Women's Erotica 2011* and *Best Bondage Erotica 2011* (both from Cleis Press). She blogs at janineashbless.blogspot.com.

DEBORAH CASTELLANO (deborahmcastellano.com) made her romantica debut in Violet Blue's *Best Women's Erotica 2009* and has also been published with Freya's Bower. When she isn't instigating mini revolutions, she is a freelance and smut writer as well as a crafter with a specialty in hand dyed and hand spun yarn.

HEIDI CHAMPA has been published in numerous anthologies including *Best Women's Erotica 2010; Playing With Fire; Please, Sir; Please, Ma'am* and *Ultimate Curves*. She has steamed up the pages of *Bust* Magazine, and her work can be found at Clean Sheets, Ravenous Romance, Oysters and Chocolate and The Erotic Woman. Find her online at heidichampa. blogspot.com.

ELIZABETH COLDWELL lives and writes in London. Her stories have appeared in numerous anthologies including *Yes, Sir*; *Please, Sir* and *Please, Ma'am*. She can be found at The (Really) Naughty Corner, elizabethcoldwell.wordpress.com, where naked waiters are never very far away.

JUSTINE ELYOT started writing for fun in 2006 and had her first story published by Black Lace in 2009. Since then, she has produced two books, numerous novellas, and short stories for publishers including Black Lace, Cleis Press, Xcite Books, Total E-Bound and Noble Romance. Contact: justineelyot.com.

EMERALD's erotic fiction has been published in numerous print and e-book anthologies as well as at various erotic websites. She is an advocate for sexual freedom, reproductive choice and sex worker rights and blogs about these and other topics at her website, thegreenlightdistrict.org.

NEIL GAVRIEL lives in the Pacific Northwest where he writes short stories of many different stripes, cooks amazing meals for his friends (who wonder why he isn't making his living as a chef) and imagines very naughty uses for superpowers.

ARIEL GRAHAM lives in Nevada with her husband and far too many cats. She can often be found doing exactly what she's not supposed to be doing while procrastinating about everything else. Her work can be found in Cleis Press anthologies, and on Pink Flamingo and Torquere.

KAY JAYBEE wrote the erotic anthologies *Quick Kink 1, Quick Kink 2*, and *The Collector*. A regular contributor to oystersand-chocolate.com, Kay also has stories published by Cleis Press, Black Lace, Mammoth, Xcite and Penguin. Details of her work can be found at kayjaybee.me.uk.

D. L. KING writes smut in New York. The editor of anthologies such as *Carnal Machines, Spank!* and *The Sweetest Kiss*, her stories can be found in *Best Women's Erotica, Best Lesbian Erotica, Mammoth Book of Best New Erotica, Fast Girls* and *Women in Lust*, among others. Find her at dlkingerotica. blogspot.com.

MADLYN MARCH is the pseudonym of a freelance journalist and erotica writer. Her stories have appeared in anthologies such as *Peep Show* and *Do Not Disturb*. She enjoys international cuisine and disco.

TERESA NOELLE ROBERTS writes romantic erotica and erotic romance for lusty people who believe in true love. Her short fiction has appeared in *Passion: Erotica for Women; Best Bondage Erotica 2011; Orgasmic; Spanked; Playing with Fire* and other anthologies. She writes erotic romance, mostly of a paranormal bent, for Samhain and Phaze.

LISABET SARAI has published six erotic novels, two short-story collections and dozens of individual tales. She also edits the single-author charity series "Coming Together Presents" and reviews erotica for Erotica Readers and Writers Association and Erotica Revealed. Visit Lisabet online at Lisabet's Fantasy Factory (lisabetsarai.com).

ANGELA R. SARGENTI writes erotic and horror stories. She has been published at Leo Degraunce, Every Night Erotica, and For the Girls, among others. She lives in California with her husband and cats and is a big fan of the Oakland A's. You may contact her at angiesargenti@yahoo.com.

SINCLAIR SEXSMITH runs the award-winning personal online writing project *Sugarbutch Chronicles: The Gender and Relationship Adventures of a Kinky Queer Butch Top* at sugarbutch.net. Mr. Sexsmith's work has appeared in various anthologies, including the *Best Lesbian Erotica* series, *Sometimes She Lets Me: Butch/Femme Erotica* and *Visible: A Femmethology* Volume 2.

CHARLOTTE STEIN has published many stories in various anthologies, including *Fairy Tale Lust*. Her own collection of shorts was named one of the best erotic romances of 2009 by Michelle Buonfiglio. She also has novellas out with Ellora's Cave, Total-E-Bound and Xcite, and you can contact her here: themightycharlottestein.blogspot.com.

KATHLEEN TUDOR is a writer from the Bay Area in California. She writes nonfiction for her day job, steamy fiction at night, and blogs about polyamory at Polyspace.wordpress.com. She works to bring a greater awareness of polyamory to the masses. Her work has been published by Circlet Press and TheEroticWoman.com.

SALOME WILDE and **TALON RIHAI** have written hundreds of thousands of words of kinky pansexual erotica together and tested out as much as possible in the flesh. Their erotic teamwork can also be found in Rachel Kramer Bussel's *Curvy Girls*.

ABOUT
THE EDITOR

RACHEL KRAMER BUSSEL (rachelkramerbussel.com) is a New York–based author, editor and blogger. She has edited over forty books of erotica, including *Going Down; Irresistible; Best Bondage Erotica 2011* and *2012; Gotta Have It; Obsessed; Women in Lust; Her Surrender; Orgasmic; Bottoms Up: Spanking Good Stories; Spanked; Naughty Spanking Stories from A to Z 1* and *2; Fast Girls; Smooth; Passion; The Mile High Club; Do Not Disturb; Tasting Him; Tasting Her; Please, Sir; Please, Ma'am; He's on Top; She's on Top; Caught Looking; Hide and Seek; Crossdressing and Rubber Sex.* She is *Best Sex Writing* series editor, and winner of 6 IPPY (Independent Publisher) Awards. Her work has been published in over one hundred anthologies, including *Best American Erotica 2004* and *2006; Zane's Chocolate Flava 2* and *Purple Panties; Everything You Know About Sex Is Wrong; Single State of the Union* and *Desire: Women Write About Wanting.* She wrote the popular "Lusty Lady" column for The *Village Voice.*

Rachel is a sex columnist for SexisMagazine.com and has written for *AVN, Bust,* Cleansheets.com, *Cosmopolitan, Curve,* The Daily Beast, Fresh Yarn, TheFrisky.com, Gothamist, Huffington Post, Mediabistro, *Newsday, New York Post, Penthouse, Playgirl, Radar,* The Root, *San Francisco Chronicle, Time Out New York* and *Zink,* among others. She has appeared on "The Martha Stewart Show," "The Berman and Berman Show," NY1 and Showtime's "Family Business." She hosted the popular In the Flesh Erotic Reading Series (inthefleshreadingseries.com), featuring readers from Susie Bright to Zane, and speaks at conferences, does readings and teaches erotic writing workshops across the country. She blogs at lustylady.blogspot.com.

Find out more about this book at anythingforyoubook.com.

Printed in the United States
by Baker & Taylor Publisher Services